The Chinese operative pointed his weapon at Bolan

The Executioner fired three times, the .44 slugs tearing into the driver's head and chest, erasing forever the hostile expression on his face.

One of the rear doors of the van opened on squealing, bent hinges. Bolan used the smoking van for cover as two other operatives, one with a Kalashnikov, one with a Makarov pistol, opened fire from either side. Bolan dived left, catching the man with the pistol. The .44 hollowpoint from the Desert Eagle tore through the man's arm lengthwise, shattering bone and digging a furrow through the flesh. The operative shrieked and stumbled, clawing at his ruined arm.

As he stepped away and around the van to the left, Bolan kept the vehicle between himself and the Kalashnikov gunner. Several bullets burned past him, high and wide, as the gunman shot blindly in Bolan's direction.

Too late, Bolan recognized the ruse. The gunner at the van had kept Bolan occupied. When the shooting stopped, Bolan heard a woman scream.

"Do not fire or you hit this woman!" one of the Chinese agents shouted.

There was nothing the Executioner could do.

MACK BOLAN ®
The Executioner

The Executioner®
Don Pendleton's
VIGILANTE RUN

A GOLD EAGLE BOOK FROM
WORLDWIDE®

TORONTO • NEW YORK • LONDON
AMSTERDAM • PARIS • SYDNEY • HAMBURG
STOCKHOLM • ATHENS • TOKYO • MILAN
MADRID • WARSAW • BUDAPEST • AUCKLAND

First edition September 2007

ISBN-13: 978-0-373-64346-2
ISBN-10:   0-373-64346-2

Special thanks and acknowledgment to
Phil Elmore for his contribution to this work.

VIGILANTE RUN

Printed in U.S.A.

Revenge is a confession of pain.

—Latin Proverb

No one understands revenge—righteous, justified revenge—better than me. But when a man crosses the line and causes deliberate harm to the innocent, he becomes just another predator and he must be stopped.

—Mack Bolan

THE
MACK BOLAN

LEGEND

Nothing less than a war could have fashioned the destiny of the man called Mack Bolan. Bolan earned the Executioner title in the jungle hell of Vietnam.

But this soldier also wore another name—Sergeant Mercy. He was so tagged because of the compassion he showed to wounded comrades-in-arms and Vietnamese civilians.

Mack Bolan's second tour of duty ended prematurely when he was given emergency leave to return home and bury his family, victims of the Mob. Then he declared a one-man war against the Mafia.

He confronted the Families head-on from coast to coast, and soon a hope of victory began to appear. But Bolan had broken society's every rule. That same society started gunning for this elusive warrior—to no avail.

So Bolan was offered amnesty to work within the system against terrorism. This time, as an employee of Uncle Sam, Bolan became Colonel John Phoenix. With a command center at Stony Man Farm in Virginia, he and his new allies—Able Team and Phoenix Force—waged relentless war on a new adversary: the KGB.

But when his one true love, April Rose, died at the hands of the Soviet terror machine, Bolan severed all ties with Establishment authority.

Now, after a lengthy lone-wolf struggle and much soul-searching, the Executioner has agreed to enter an "arm's-length" alliance with his government once more, reserving the right to pursue personal missions in his Everlasting War.

Camillus, New York

The hollow-core wooden door cracked and fell inward as Mack Bolan kicked it off its hinges. He stepped over the shattered particleboard, the barrel of his Beretta 93-R machine pistol leading the way. He swept left and right, his support hand gripping a small but powerful combat light and tracking with the pistol. The white beam illuminated the debris within the ramshackle trailer. The place was a mess and smelled worse than it looked. It stank of decay and reeked heavily of ammonia. The Executioner's eyes watered as he stepped forward into the darkness.

The mobile home was a dump in more ways than one. The "lawn" outside was little more than mud dotted with weeds. Behind and on both sides of the moldy trailer, piles of garbage told the soldier exactly what he was about to find. Empty cans of paint thinner were stacked four and five high together with jugs of industrial chemicals, mostly hydrochloric and muriatic acid. There were other drums and barrels that he could not identify, and several broken wooden shipping pallets.

The refuse outside, piled ten feet high in some places, had smelled bad enough exposed to the open air; in the close quarters of the mobile home it was suffocating. A card table toppled as Bolan brushed past it. Dozens of empty cardboard boxes of generic dollarstore sinus and cold medicine fell to the floor.

Wading through the shin-high rubbish strewed on the floor—empty mason jars, spent bottles of camp-stove fuel, cigarette butts, fast-food wrappers and more bulging bags of rotting garbage—Bolan tore away one of the black plastic trash bags taped over the nearest window. The glass was filthy and cracked, but through it he could see waning twilight. The stars above the snow-covered field would have been pretty if seen anywhere else. Here, they were only a backdrop against which to contrast man's viciousness.

Bolan found the first body not far from the window.

The dead man was dressed in filthy denims under a leather biker jacket. He was covered in blood. The top of his head was gone and Bolan could not determine through the gore how old he might have been. Toeing the corpse over with the edge of his combat boot, the soldier got a good look at the logo on the back of the jacket: CNY Purists. He hadn't heard of that one before. Slipping a tiny digital camera from a slit pocket of his blacksuit, Bolan snapped a couple of shots of the symbol, a stylized and fairly typical skull and snake surrounded by the letters of the gang's name. The team at Stony Man Farm would be able to turn up intel on the group.

In the debris, Bolan almost missed the gun. The Colt Python was sticky with congealing blood. He left it there. The owner wouldn't be needing it and evidence gathering was best left to the local police. Bolan was no cop, and he wasn't there to tag and bag the obvious.

The floor creaked as the man in black made his way down the narrow hallway joining the trailer's living room to what he presumed was once a bedroom. There was less garbage. The space was full of camp stoves, bottles of drain cleaner and a mess of tangled plastic tubing, metal drums and broken glass. The ammonia fumes were so intense that Bolan had to back out of the room. As he did so, the beam of his flashlight played across the bullet holes pocking the bare, water-damaged drywall.

There was a second bedroom at the end of the hall. It was a wreck like the rest of the trailer, but with more domestic debris. The litter was mostly dirty clothes and empty liquor bottles. A sawed-off pump shotgun, jacked open and empty, was lying on the floor amid a pile of fired plastic shells. Bolan's light showed buckshot peppering the walls and even the floor in the bedroom and hallway. There were several more bullet holes here, too, large enough to be .44 or .45 slugs.

Two more bodies were sprawled on the floor. One was a long-haired, shirtless male wearing leather pants and engineer's boots. The other was a half-naked woman. She was stretched out at the foot of a baby's crib.

Bolan's jaw tightened. The crib was missing slats from its railings and was covered in peeling paint. It was shoved against the wall under the room's single window, the only one in the trailer not covered with black plastic. One leg was broken; it was propped on a broken piece of cinder block. There were bloodstained blankets inside.

In the center of the railing, the wooden spokes had been blasted apart, leaving a larger hole lined in splintered and broken dowels. The wall beyond the crib, visible through the slats on the far side, was dotted with three more large bullet holes.

The woman on the floor in front of the crib clutched a .38 snubnose revolver in lifeless fingers. She was emaciated, with deep, dark circles under her eyes. From what Bolan could see, she was toothless. Her chest was covered in blood and she'd taken multiple shots. Bolan pried the .38 from her grasp, his gloved thumb pushing the cylinder release and snapping it open. There were no indentations on the primers. She'd never gotten off a shot.

Steeling himself, the soldier rose and stepped closer to the crib.

The baby had taken at least one slug, maybe two.

Blue eyes hard with anger, Bolan stared down at the innocent life cut short by violence. He turned—

The window shattered. Something heavy and metallic bounced across the unmade and bloodstained bed before clattering to the floor.

The hand grenade rolled to a stop at Bolan's feet.

His eyes widened. Without hesitation, the soldier threw himself out the already broken window, tumbling though the mud and slush and crashing through a stack of empty paint-thinner cans. Ignoring the noise of the falling containers, he ran as fast as he could pump his legs, doomsday numbers falling as he put most of a snow-covered and weed-chocked field between himself and the mobile home.

The muffled thump of the grenade—an incendiary,

Bolan realized—was followed almost immediately by a series of deafening explosions. Waves of heat rolled over Bolan. The mobile home became an instant funeral pyre, its volatile contents consuming themselves and everything within the trailer as chemicals and cooking equipment went up in flames.

"He's there! He's there!"

Prone, Bolan whipped his head to the side as a shot rang out, digging a furrow not six inches from where his face had been. He rolled and got up, the Beretta still clutched in his fist. He'd lost his flashlight in the mad dash from the mobile home. Sighting on the muzzle-flashes, he drilled a series of 3-round bursts into the night. One of his unseen opponents cried out.

"Benny! Benny, you okay?" demanded the voice.

Whomever Benny might be, he was out of the action. Bolan was already moving, the noise of his steps drowned by the crackling fires eating the meth lab. There were at least three of them, plus the unfortunate Benny. They were fanning out, backlit by the dancing flames.

Bolan took careful aim and tapped out a single 3-round burst, tagging one of the moving figures in the head. The other two fired in his direction—one with a handgun, the other with a machine pistol of some kind. The stuttering of the full-auto zipper followed Bolan into the darkness. It was a 9 mm, most likely; probably a micro-Uzi or an Ingram. Bolan doubted a single round had come near him. The threat came from the aimed fire to his left, from the man who'd called out to Benny. The speaker's partner was the spray-and-pray type.

As the deepening night filled more space between

Bolan and the burning drug lab, he circled, flanking his pursuers. The two men were stumbling blindly after him. It would be easy to take them both, but he needed answers. That meant trying to get one of them alive.

"Carver! I don't see him!" It was a different voice, the voice of the man with the machine pistol.

"Shut the fuck up, Stick," Carver barked. "Watch for movement and then—"

It was good advice and Bolan took it, emptying his Beretta into Carver. The man went down without a sound. Another wild burst of Parabellum rounds went wide of him as Stick reacted. Shoving the empty Beretta into his web belt, Bolan dropped to his left knee, drawing his .44 Magnum Desert Eagle from the tactical thigh holster on his right leg. The gas-fed hand cannon thundered as Bolan triggered two boattail rounds low and left. The first one missed, but the second took Stick in the abdomen. The thug's knees buckled and he dropped to the ground.

Fishing in a pouch of his web belt, Bolan produced a small LED backup light. He held the little aluminum cylinder between the fingers of his left hand as he advanced on Stick, Desert Eagle at the ready. Stick was moaning and rocking slightly, clutching at his guts with both arms wrapped tightly around his stomach as he knelt doubled over and sobbing. Not far away, steaming in the snow, was Stick's fallen MAC-10, the bolt closed.

"You son of a bitch," he blubbered.

Stick was a lanky man of thirty to forty years with greasy shoulder-length hair and a face like a rodent's. His chin was covered in a scraggly growth that made him look even more like a rat. In the blue-tinted glare of his pocket light, Bolan could see the logo on Stick's sleeveless denim shirt—CNY Purists.

"Talk," Bolan said simply.

Stick looked up accusingly. "What the fuck do you want?" he wheezed.

"I want to know what happened here."

"You should goddamned know well enough what you done here, you bastard," Stick sputtered. "You killed Chopper Mike! You killed his old lady! You killed their freaking *kid,* man. Why would you do that? Who *are* you?"

"Start from the beginning," Bolan commanded. The triangular nose of the Desert Eagle never wavered. Hugging himself, Stick squinted at the man in black and appeared to look him up and down.

"I ain't telling you nothing," he whimpered. His voice hardened. "I ain't telling nothing to no tall, dark-haired badass dressed like a commando who just hit our place on Route 173."

Bolan's eyes grew wide again. He pistoned a vicious straight kick into the biker, sending him sprawling. There was a lot of blood, but Stick wasn't wounded as badly as he'd let on. The wireless phone he'd been hiding—and into which he'd been speaking for someone's benefit—landed in the snow a few feet away.

Growling like an animal, Stick surged to his feet. The serrated blade of a folding knife flashed in the beam of Bolan's light. As the biker lunged, Bolan fired twice. Stick was dead before what was left of him settled wetly into the snow.

The Executioner retrieved the phone, a cheap and untraceable prepaid unit. The connection was still open. As his thumb went for the "status" button, the call was terminated from the other end. The local number Stick had dialed was the only one in the phone's call log. Looking at the dead man and then glancing back in Carver's direction, Bolan shook his head. For meth-running bikers, they were far from stupid. Still, he at least had a few clues to feed to the Farm.

As the meth lab continued to burn, Bolan heard the first of the sirens approaching.

Stony Man Farm, Virginia

AS BARBARA PRICE ENTERED Stony Man Farm's computer room, nose wrinkling at the smell from the pot of industrial-strength coffee warming on a nearby countertop, she had to dodge Aaron "The Bear" Kurtzman as he rolled by.

"Hal's waiting on the scrambler and I've got work to do," Kurtzman said, wheeling past and circling her in his chair as he transferred a memory stick from one computer to another, juggling a handful of processed satellite images and doing it all while holding a beer-stein-size coffee mug. The barrel-chested computer expert gestured with one massive forearm toward the communications gear at the far end of the room.

Smiling, Stony Man's honey-blond, model-beautiful mission controller stepped past him. Kurtzman always got grumpy when he was short staffed. The rest of his team was on leave or at conferences in various parts of the States, leaving him to field most of their duties during a mercifully light week free of nation-endangering crises. There was more than a little humor to that, Price reflected; Kurtzman had suffered without complaint the injury that had left him a paraplegic for life—but he got testy when asked to answer the phone too often.

The man from Justice was waiting for her on the satellite feed. Though Hal Brognola didn't appear too worried at the moment, Price knew it was only a matter of time before the big Fed would be forced to fight yet another looming disaster. The fact that he hadn't come to the Farm in person was a promising sign. He'd have shown up in person if there were serious problems, Price thought.

"Barb," Brognola said.

"Hal," Price acknowledged, sitting down and holding the headset to her ear without putting it on. "What can we do for you?"

"It's not me, at least not directly," Brognola said. When Price did not comment, he continued. "I asked Striker to look into something that's had Justice very concerned for the past two months."

"Something we're tracking?" Price asked, though she knew that was not likely.

"Too vague for that. We've been getting reports through Homeland Security of what was supposed to be terrorism, or isolated events that at least *looked* like terrorism. I did some checking and what I found was a series of murders across central New York."

"Nothing new about that," Price said evenly.

"No, nothing new about that," Brognola admitted. "These were disturbing, though. A family and several others killed in a home in Skaneateles. Three cops shot in Syracuse. A string of arsons in a suburb of the city that claimed the lives of four children and at least three adults. On the surface they're the usual crimes, though the rate is a lot higher for an upstate city that sees maybe twenty homicides in a normal year. We almost missed it."

"Missed what?" Price asked.

"The pattern," the big Fed said with a frown. "Larry Kearney is a contact of mine, used to be a reporter here in D.C. He runs a think tank in central New York now and has his hands in a local alternative paper. He spends his time doing what got him run out of Wonderland in the first place—pissing off politicians and raking muck."

Price laughed. "He sounds like your kind of person."

"More or less." Brognola managed a faint grin. "It was Larry who put me on the trail. The murder victims—those who weren't collateral damage—were all connected to the local methamphetamine trade. At least, that's what Larry believes. He didn't have much more to go on."

"Why involve Justice?" Price asked. "Wouldn't this be a matter for the local police?"

"It might be," Brognola said grimly, "if not for Larry's nose for corruption. He suspects collusion with local law enforcement. This isn't simply drug dealers taking shots at the competition, either. He tells me, and I believe him, that there's something more methodical at work."

"A vigilante?" Price raised an eyebrow.

"That's Larry's theory. Given the brutality of the crimes and the alphabet soup of government agencies in which Syracuse is now swimming, it's a circus. He called me to call in a favor. He said he thought I could cut through some of the red tape and produce results."

"That's a lot to ask of a man in your position."

"Not if you know Larry," Brognola said. "He was one of the best sources of insider information I had here. He knew where all the bodies were buried. That's what made him enemies here—powerful enemies. I owe him. So I asked Striker to investigate."

Price nodded. Who better to track a vigilante than Mack Bolan? Bolan had what was at times an arm's-length relationship with the Farm, but the staff's commitment to him, and his to them individually, was unwavering. She considered the man for a moment. Where was he? What was he doing? Price had an off-again, on-again relationship with the soldier. Neither of them asked for more than the other could give. It was enough. Still, she worried for him, when she let herself.

"What can we do?" Price asked. If the Farm could assist Bolan, she'd see to it.

"I'm relaying specifications he transmitted to me through his scrambled phone," Brognola said, typing at his computer beyond the view of the sat link. "He needs a care package from you guys."

"We'll do our best to fill his wish list," Price nodded.

"I also need Bear and his team to dig up anything and everything they can find on a biker gang called the CNY Purists. I'm sending a digital shot Striker took during a raid on one of their facilities last night that might help. You can send the data directly to him through his wireless."

"We'll get on it, Hal."

"Thanks." He moved to cut the connection.

"Hal?" Price asked.

Brognola paused.

"When you talk to him, tell him to look after himself."

"I will," Brognola promised. He cut the feed.

Price stared at the blank screen for a moment before turning to examine the incoming data. There was work to be done.

Camillus, New York

THE EXECUTIONER LEANED against the black-and-white Syracuse police car, his arms folded across his chest. He'd spent a long night telling and retelling his story, doing his best to wear out the Justice credentials Brognola had provided in the name of Agent Matt Cooper. Now he was simply waiting for the all clear so he could resume his work.

The delay was annoying, but necessary. He would need the cooperation of local law enforcement, and he needed to know who the federal players were. In addition, making himself known might shake loose whomever Brognola's source believed was cooperating with the murderer or murderers Bolan sought. If he made a big enough target of himself, it was a sure bet someone would take a crack at him to get him out of the way.

At least three government agencies were represented—DEA, FBI and ATF—while the county sheriff's office and two neighboring police districts had sent units, as well. Bolan had waited patiently while they worked through their histrionics and exaggerated outrage at his presence. One of the ATF agents had held the Beretta 93-R by two fingers as if examining a venomous snake; the FBI duo had threatened to haul him in for interrogation if his ID and story didn't hold up. The city and suburban police had steered clear of him but shot him suspicious looks. About the only one of them Bolan didn't immediately dislike was a rookie named Paglia, who watched him carefully but expressed no emotion. That one had the look of a decent lawman who, if he stayed on the force and kept his wits about him, would go far, Bolan thought. He'd seen the type. He'd seen the opposite, too.

When their phone calls and computer queries came back verifying Cooper's affiliation with the Justice Department, the squawking had largely stopped. Bolan was, however, obliged to stick around until cleared to leave, if he didn't want to burn any bridges. The mobile home had long since burned itself out, and the agents and police were busily picking through the smoldering debris.

Officer Paglia, who looked impossibly young to Bolan despite his air of competence, returned to his car to drop off several evidence bags. They contained shell casings and a few other odds and ends. Bolan did not expect any of the departments involved to turn up much of use from the burned wreckage, but there was always a chance.

Paglia also carried with him Bolan's leather shoulder harness, in which was slung the 93-R and its spare magazines. He handed the harness to Bolan and then, from behind his belt, produced the Desert Eagle. "They say you can have your roscoes back," Paglia chuckled. "They weren't too happy about it."

"I'm surprised they let you take any of the evidence," Bolan commented, nodding at the agents in their variously lettered windbreakers.

"There's enough to go around," Paglia told him. Something caught his eye as he turned from his vehicle. He bent to retrieve a singed and empty cardboard carton. Several more just like it were scattered across the field, hurled there by the explosion. The agents and police officers had been walking on them for most of the night.

"Cold medicine," he said.

"Pseudoephedrine," Bolan told him. "It's a precursor chemical, cooked from the over-the-counter drugs in order to manufacture methamphetamine."

"Crystal meth," the cop said. "This is a drug house?"

"It used to be," Bolan said.

FROM THE TREE LINE ACROSS the snow-covered field, Gary Rook watched the big man in black collect his things and return to the unmarked Chevy Blazer in which he'd arrived the previous night. Through the powerful scope of the Remington 700, the dark-haired man's face was clearly visible. Rook did his best to memorize the intruder's features. He had a feeling they would meet again, soon.

Rook had watched as the commando rolled up and entered the meth lab. There was something very unusual about the interloper. He moved like Rook himself—like a man who knew his way around a battlefield. His armed entry into the trailer was textbook, though Rook could have told him there was no one alive in the trailer.

The big, bearded man smiled through red-orange whiskers. His forearms tightened as he flexed his fingers on the synthetic stock of the Remington. Briefly he had considered putting a .308 slug through the commando's head, but he'd decided to wait. It was a very informative delay. When the Purists arrived, more or less silently on foot, he assumed they'd walked in from wherever they'd left their vehicles, responding to some desperate call made from within the trailer before Rook had finished dealing with the occupants. He'd written off the newcomer then, only to watch in surprise as the man finished each of the bikers in turn. By the time the cops began to show it was too late to move without alerting them to his presence, so he stayed where he was. He watched as they detained the commando, went through their usual songs and dances, then grudgingly turned loose the man in black. Whoever he was, he had powerful connections to go with the ordnance he was packing.

The commando was rolling out in his SUV. Rook resigned himself to waiting until the police and the Feds cleared out, as well. Then he'd make his way back to his own truck and plan his next strike. He'd steer clear of the man in black if he could. If not, well, that was too bad.

If necessary, Rook would kill him, just like the others.

2

Syracuse, New York

Roger Kohler was a busy man. As CEO and majority shareholder of Diamond Corporation, Kohler shepherded an empire spanning everything from low-income rental properties throughout Syracuse, to paid city parking lots, to a piece of the Salt City's inner harbor development area. He owned three of New York State's six largest shopping malls—though not, much to his chagrin, one in the city itself. He was working to change that; he was brokering a deal to build the largest shopping mall yet in the state, on the city's south side.

The project was not without its detractors. The Supreme Court had done him the favor of ruling that local governments could seize property for private investors if that property could be used to generate more revenue. Ostensibly that was for the "public good." Whatever the justification, this *de facto* elimination of private property worked to Kohler's advantage—or it would, once he got approval to seize a large enough chunk of the city's southwest quarter. It had been done before. One of Kohler's competitors, another major property concern, had successfully muscled out two dozen established businesses in the city to erect a high-priced luxury hotel that had yet to turn a profit. With that precedent set, Kohler expected only token resistance to his new mall. If legitimate companies could be shown the door in the name of higher tax revenues, who would care about a handful of drug addicts and gang members living in the city's biggest slum?

Listen to any radio or television newscast in Syracuse and the words "There was a shooting today" or "There was a stabbing today" would be immediately followed by the phrase "on the south side." Every American city had such a place, if not more than one—an overwhelmingly poor ghetto wherein most of the local crime and the criminals committing it could be found. What better place to clear away for dynamic economic development, for commerce? Kohler couldn't imagine why everyone in the city didn't embrace the idea.

There was squawking from the local activist groups, of course. These included wealthy liberals consumed with guilt about their own success, neighborhood sign-wavers belonging to political action and protest organizations, and a scattered few local politicians who had refused to join Kohler's unofficial payroll. They wouldn't stop him. Those who couldn't be marginalized or ignored could simply be eliminated. Kohler maintained certain "business contacts" for that purpose.

Those were not the only problems. There were those who said the city's depressed economy—the natural outcome of a state whose taxes consistently ranked it among the highest in the nation—couldn't support such a large project. They didn't see the opportunities for tourism that Kohler and Diamond promised. They didn't see the sales tax revenues his consumer and community development center offered. There were those who claimed the city was still reeling from his competitor's failure to successfully implement the competitor's own pie-in-the-sky dreams of consumer paradise.

It didn't help that the failed project—a tremendous mall expansion included absurd plans for everything from a water park and amusement center to a monorail linking the expanded facility to downtown Syracuse—was irrevocably coupled in the minds of locals to a series of bizarre publicity stunts.

Kohler had himself helped sink the project to make way for his own plans, though he regretted just how well it had worked. His own operatives had signed on for the supposed jobs that were created during the project's opening stages, doing everything from enforcing mall curfew policies to cleaning up area subsidized homes in a bid to perform community service busywork. He made sure that his operatives were among those kept most discreetly in his employ—those who had criminal records. Then he leaked the records to the local newspaper, whose editorial board gleefully reported both the busywork and the felonies. The resulting public relations nightmare put an end to Kohler's competitor's dream of revitalizing the city. That left Kohler in what was supposed to have been the perfect position to take up the slack.

The problem was that Kohler's own project was losing money every day and didn't seem likely to break even once ground was broken and construction started. The business plan simply wasn't viable, and Kohler knew it. He could not and would not accept failure, however. That left him with only one option—supplementing his business plan off the books with income from another source.

Kohler was a realist. He had no family. He had no gods. He had only one goal, and that was to enrich himself. He was perfectly at ease with this fact. If it meant he had to consort with a certain class of people, so be it. They were necessary as long as they were useful. They were also easily removed once they *stopped* being useful.

It was with this thought in mind that Kohler told his secretary to admit Gerald "Pick" McWilliams. It was extremely unusual for Mr. McWilliams to show his face in the Kohler Towers. It was, in fact, forbidden, as far as Kohler was concerned. Only a matter of extreme urgency could bring McWilliams here. Only the severity of Kohler's financial situation prompted him to permit such an intrusion.

McWilliams came dressed in a thrift store tweed suit that was at least a size too large for him, complete with a polyester tie as thick as a scarf that had to have dated back to the 1970s. The secretary admitted him without a word, and McWilliams almost managed to restrain a leer. Under other circumstances, Kohler would have had trouble blaming the man, as he'd hired Lori specifically to look good. She was blond, she looked great in a tight white blouse, and she never wore skirts longer than midcalf. She was even a passable typist. Mostly, however, she simply guarded the portal to Kohler's domain and impressed anyone who came calling.

"Pick," Kohler said without preamble, "what the hell are you doing here?"

McWilliams was a mouse of a man, thin and gaunt, missing a few teeth and suffering from questionable personal hygiene. He was Kohler's go-between to the CNY Purists, a crude but effective local gang that had proved to be very useful in the less legal aspects of Diamond's operations. McWilliams was easily intimidated, which was why Kohler tolerated him.

Roger Kohler was formidable enough in his own right. He stood three inches over six feet tall and had the thick build to show for the hours spent in his private gymnasium. He was also a third-degree black belt in karate, the knuckles of his hands scarred and thick from punching bricks and breaking boards. Though his silver hair was growing sparse, Kohler's granite-hard features left no doubt that he was a man in his physical prime who had no qualms about crushing anyone who got in his way. Kohler permitted himself the visual fantasy of throwing an edge-of-hand strike into McWilliams's throat simply for being beneath him.

"Mr. Kohler, sir." McWilliams practically bowed and scraped as he spoke. "There's a…a problem with the shipment."

"A problem."

"Yes, sir."

"With the shipment."

"Yes, sir," McWilliams confirmed again.

"Would you mind telling me, Pick, *just what the fuck I pay you people for?*"

Kohler came around from behind the desk, grabbing McWilliams by his wide lapels. "You and your friends have exactly one job to do, and that is to see that the product reaches Ithaca by Sunday! You have exactly five days to meet that deadline. If you do not, we have a serious problem. I will most certainly kill you, but I will have to get in line behind the Chinese and I'll have to do it before *they* kill *me!*"

"It's not my fault!" McWilliams whined, making no attempt to protect himself as Kohler shook him like a dog worrying a chew toy. "They hit the cook house we were using. All the product's gone and the place was blown to shit! We lost a lot of guys, man. You don't know!"

Kohler paused and released McWilliams, straightening his own suit as he took a deep breath. *"That,"* he told McWilliams, "is precisely why I pay you and your fellow miscreants. These things happen. Straighten it out. Have a turf war, or something. Do whatever it is you people do. I don't care who you have to kill. Just do it. Make the problem go away and make damned sure the shipment is all there, on time, by Sunday. Otherwise I swear I'll break every bone in your body before Chang and his people get to *me.*"

McWilliams nodded so hard that Kohler thought the unctuous little man's head might snap off. The middle-man scuttled away without another word, leaving Kohler to consider his empty office, his empty bank accounts and his very full schedule. He decided, then and there, that outside help was in order. He paused to bring up a few relevant files on his computer, including everything he had on McWilliams and his key associates. Then he accessed several of his confidential files. If the Purists couldn't get the job done, he would bring in someone who could.

While he was at it, he'd see to it that McWilliams was erased simply for annoying him one time too many. McWilliams's medical records contained an interesting fact. He'd pass that along in the spirit of cooperation. With luck, his new consultant could speed up the process and Kohler could get his business ventures back on track all the sooner.

Despite what he'd told McWilliams, he knew it was unlikely they'd make Chang's shipment deadline. Given that, he'd have to make alternate arrangements, and given Chang's difficult temperament, he'd have to make them himself.

Kohler sighed.

It was so hard to get good help these days.

Armory Square, Syracuse

THE INTERIOR OF THE Tyrannosaur Barbecue was dark, crowded and loud, just the way Trogg Sharpe liked it. The massive leader of the CNY Purists held court there almost every day, seated at a plank table in the far corner of his domain with a plate of suicide wings or hot-sauced spareribs in front of him. There was always a row of gleaming chromed motorcycles parked in front of the Tyrannosaur, which had been a Syracuse landmark for more than thirty years. At any given time, at least half of those bikes belonged to the CNY Purists, central New York's largest and most brutal motorcycle club.

Sharpe's bulk was as much fat as muscle. His tremendous belly distended the black Live to Ride T-shirt he wore under a leather vest sporting plenty of chain and the Purist's colors. Still, he was no one to test lightly. Sharpe had put his fair share of men in hospitals with nothing more than his ham-size hands. At five foot eight and well over three hundred pounds, he lumbered slowly and inexorably through life, confident in the power of the Purists and in the damage he could do through sheer viciousness. The biker demanded relatively little of life—good booze, the occasional smoke. He liked a willing woman from time to time, the younger the better. Apart from that, he was content— as long as nobody got in his way. Those who did he beat down. Any man or woman who messed with him learned never to test him again. Or they died.

Sharpe smiled as he worked his way through a plate of ribs, reaching out and trying to grab the leatherskirted waitress as she clicked by on stiletto heels. She told him to screw himself and kept walking. Sharpe laughed. The Tyrannosaur was known for its great barbecue and its lousy, rude service. It was a tradition. He wiped hot sauce from his bushy beard with the back of his hand and reached for his beer amid the empties already collecting on the table.

The other Purists in attendance were circulating through the room, some eating at tables of their own, others engaged in a game of poker in the back room.

Sharpe planned to join the poker game when he was finished eating. First things first.

Snapper, Sharpe's third in command, was examining the jukebox across the room. He stared at the scarred glass box as if his life depended on the song he picked. Jesus, but it took Snapper forever to make a decision. Sharpe had just about run out of patience and was getting ready to demand something by CCR.

His world exploded.

One moment he was watching as the front door of the place opened—he saw the silhouette of a big man in dark clothing against the almost blinding light of day outside the darkened barbecue shack. The next moment, he was falling backward in his chair, a deafening roar in his ears as lightning bolts danced in front of his dimming vision. He hit the floor, but did not feel it. For Sharpe, everything that ever was disappeared into pain and brightness and then nothing.

BOLAN, IN HIS RENTED Blazer, pulled away from the drop point. A heavy war bag sat in the passenger seat, its zippers pulled open to reveal the cache of equipment and weapons within. The Farm's gunsmith, John "Cowboy" Kissinger, had done his usual excellent work, from the look of things. The men and women at the Farm had filled his gear requests and had even thrown in a few extras.

One of the items Bolan had specifically asked for was a portable police scanner, programmed with the appropriate local frequencies. Another was a handheld GPS unit. If he was to track a murderer in unfamiliar

territory—territory his quarry knew, presumably—
Bolan would need a technological edge. He'd learned
well in battlefields across the globe that terrain, and
knowledge of it, could make all the difference in an
armed conflict.

Bolan switched on the scanner and set it to rotate
through its presets automatically. Almost immediately,
it came to life with an excited voice: "…I say again,
shots fired, shots fired, Tyrannosaur Barbecue, North
Willow. It sounds like a damned war! Shots fired, shots
fired…"

Bolan thumbed the GPS unit to life and checked it.
He was only blocks away.

The Blazer's tires squealed as he put the accelerator
to the floor.

GARY ROOK HAD PLANTED ONE combat boot against the
crash bar on the front door of the Tyrannosaur. He'd
kicked it in, took a single step, raised his Smith &
Wesson 625 and fired. The .45ACP hollowpoint round
thundered straight for Trogg Sharpe, bowling over the
fat man and dumping him in a corpulent heap on the
sawdust-strewn floor.

There was a moment of absolute silence as bikers,
other patrons and serving staff all turned to Rook, eyes
wide in shock.

Rook cut loose.

He methodically moved the four-inch barrel of the
big stainless-steel revolver, firing the weapon double-
action each time he found a target. A biker standing by
the jukebox was hammered into the now-shattered

glass, blood and bone flecking the shattered CDs inside the unit. Another was whipped backward as a slug tore a channel through his head, spraying brain tissue out an exit wound the size of a quarter. Rook did not hear the screaming as he dropped men and women alike, his ears ringing despite the foam earplugs he wore. As the revolver clicked empty on the seventh pull, he used his left hand to draw an identical weapon from the second of two cross-draw leather holsters at his waist. His prey began to return fire as he started cycling through another half-dozen 230-grain rounds.

The bikers were brutal enough, but they had no technique and no initiative. As long as Rook could keep them on the defensive, he knew he would win every time. He almost laughed as a stocky Purist in leather pants and a denim vest popped up from behind an overturned table—just in time for Rook to pump a round through his chest. The biker caved in on himself and Rook dropped to the floor.

Holstering his revolvers, Rook drew two full-size Rock Island Armory 1911-style .45 automatic pistols from leather shoulder holsters under both arms. Then he was up again, sparing two rounds for a crawling Purist he'd wounded through the gut with the first salvo. He stepped over a dead waitress, her hair snaking through a growing puddle of blood, and made his way to the back. There, he knew, there was almost always a card game going on.

Automatic gunfire ripped through the doorway as Rook hugged one side of the opening. There were Purists back there, all right, and they were waiting for him to stick his head in and get it shot off. Rook smiled again. From the shoulder bag hanging across his chest, he withdrew a Molotov—a simple beer bottle filled with gasoline, a gas-soaked rag plugging the neck of the bottle. He waited for a lull in the gunfire and then tossed the bottle.

"Look out!" someone shouted from the back room.

Rook whipped one hand around the doorjamb and fired the .45 dry. At least one of the rounds managed to ignite the gasoline. The *whoosh* of flame was followed by an agonized cry as one of the room's occupants began to burn. Rook risked a direct look through the doorway and fired his other .45 empty, tagging at least one cowering Purist who had not been caught by the fire. Then he backed out into the main room of the Tyrannosaur, reloading each of his .45s awkwardly as he juggled both weapons.

The crackle of fire and the sudden squealing of smoke alarms did not distract him as he stalked through the room. Something moved in the shadow of one of the booths on the far wall. Rook blasted it three times and kept going. He shouldered through the doors to the Tyrannosaur's kitchen.

"You bastard!" someone screamed. Rook jumped back and narrowly missed being slashed by the big kitchen knife, wielded by a heavy man in a dirty white T-shirt and apron. The balding, middle-aged man could only be a cook, from the look of him.

"Wait," Rook protested.

The man grunted and slashed again, driving Rook back the way he'd come. Rook shrugged mentally and shot the man center mass, watching dispassionately as he dropped his knife and fell to the floor.

That was life in the big city, wasn't it?

The police would arrive at any moment. Rook took another Molotov from his bag, lit it with a disposable lighter from his pocket and tossed it in to the center of the kitchen. It burst and tinted the scene orange. Rook could feel the searing heat on his face as he left through the kitchen's emergency exit, ignoring the alarm bell that started ringing as soon as the door opened. His truck, parked illegally in the alley behind the Tyrannosaur, was waiting for him.

He did not even spare the burning restaurant a glance in his rearview mirror as he sped away.

BOLAN SKIDDED AROUND THE corner at the Willow Street intersection, skirting the Tyrannosaur and almost sideswiping a row of parked motorcycles. He came to a halt and threw himself from the vehicle, war bag slung across his body over one shoulder. He could see flames dancing at the rear of the building as black smoke filled the sky. There was no other activity. The place was a loss, and the soldier had obviously just missed whatever had happened. Several people from neighboring businesses had come out to watch the fire and were talking animatedly to one another. Bolan could sense their eyes on him as he backed away from the building.

Bolan caught movement from the corner of his eye and turned in time to see a gigantic man, his face covered in blood, stagger from the building. He was followed by a second, much thinner man, who was cradling his arm. The smaller man's skin was lobster red. He was badly burned.

The fat man raised a .38 revolver and opened fire, screaming.

Bolan heaved himself behind the Blazer. One of the slugs tore into the fender; another blew the tire. Bolan unleathered his Beretta and prepared to bring it into play. Before he could fire, he heard the revving of a motorcycle engine.

Jumping up, the Executioner tracked the big man as the chopper squealed away, carrying both wounded men. It shot past the Blazer and toward the milling crowds on the street. The big man on the bike spared Bolan a venomous glance backward but did not fire again as he surged away. Bolan held his fire; there were too many innocents between him and the biker. The bike burned around a corner and disappeared as Bolan turned back to his Blazer and its flat front tire.

For the second time in as many days, he heard police and fire sirens in the background, headed his way. The Tyrannosaur continued to burn and he was no closer to finding the man responsible.

3

Liverpool, New York

Gary Rook was in hell.

He visited hell every night. Every night was the same as the last. In his sleep, he was terrorized by dreams of Jennifer as she'd been near the end—toothless, thinner than seemed possible, racked with spasms and tics. The haunted look in her sunken, bloodshot eyes was something he'd never forget, not for as long as he lived. There was no doubt in Rook's mind that when he finally got to hell, she would be there to meet him. Seeing her every night was simply his penance, his prepayment for the sins he had committed and would continue to commit. Only when he was on the streets, making *them* pay, could Rook feel some measure of peace, some sense of justice and satisfaction. At night, the knowledge of what he'd done weighed heavily on him. Thoughts of what Jennifer herself would think of what he was doing hurt him even more.

Rook had no illusions. He knew that what he was doing was wrong. He knew that he was doing it for himself, too—Jennifer was long past caring and nothing he did would bring her back. Rook was a murderer. He was guilty and he expected, eventually, to be caught or killed.

He didn't care.

Whipping his head to the side as he woke himself from the nightmare, Rook gasped. He blinked a few times, then brought his wristwatch to his face and tried to focus on it. It was morning, and later than he liked. He sighed. He had better waste no more time.

He sat up in the sweat-stained, tangled sheets, staring uncomprehendingly at the pillow lying on the floor near the full-size bed. The apartment was almost bare except for the bed and a few cardboard boxes stuffed with clothes and other personal items. Guns, ammunition and other supplies were strewed about the floor. There was no furniture on which to place them. Rook owned no television, either—he couldn't be bothered to spend any time in front of one.

Empty bottles of bourbon lay on their sides at the foot of the bed, next to an overflowing ashtray. Rook found his mostly crushed box of Marlboros, in which he'd stuffed another disposable lighter, and sucked to life one of the last of his cigarettes. One of his .45s, cocked and locked with a round in the chamber, lay on the sheet where it had been under his pillow. He picked it up, snapped off the safety and considered it.

He would never kill himself. He wanted to, sometimes, but not badly enough to actually do it. To be honest, it scared him. He knew where he was going and wasn't in a hurry to get there. Besides, while he was alive, he could keep killing members of the Purists. He might even be able to kill them all.

He wondered what he would do, then. But it didn't matter. It would be a long time before he got them all.

Syracuse, New York

"COME ON, JACKER," TROGG grunted, holding the blood-stained bag of ice to his aching head. "Hurry the fuck up."

"I'm doing my best, man," Jacker whined. His left arm in a sling, Jacker moved a felt-tipped marker back and forth on the dog-eared sheet of copy paper. He paused to push stringy, dirty-blond hair out of his eyes and then bent to his work again.

"Don't test me, Jacker," Trogg rumbled. He flexed the fingers of both his hands, picturing them wrapped around a throat. He wanted to find that commando. It had to be the same guy; there was no question. It was the guy who'd hit the cook house, the guy who'd butchered Chopper Mike, Mike's old lady, and even his rug rat. Trogg had done worse himself over the course of his life, but this was different. This was *family*. This was the Purists. Nobody tried to do the Purists like this son of a bitch had done. He was going to pay. Yeah, he was going to pay, but *first* he was going to *suffer*. Trogg was going to take great pleasure in torturing the bastard until he went insane—and then torturing him some more until he died.

The doctor Trogg used for these little incidents had treated him and Jacker, taken his bribe and scuttled off. Trogg almost had to laugh. It was a good bet the city's south side was the only part of Syracuse that still got house calls from the local medical establishment. Like anything in life, you could have whatever you wanted if you didn't care what it cost and you didn't care what laws you broke. Sure, a lot of the doctors paid to come by were, well, less than legitimate, but you took what you could get.

Trogg knew he was lucky to be alive. His head felt as if it were going to split open. The bullet had creased his forehead but left his skull intact, leaving him with what was going to be an impressive scar when the stitches came out. He was doped to the gills on codeine from his private stash of painkillers. Jacker had bad burns and a busted arm, but he'd recover, too. He wasn't going to be very pretty, what with the skin all screwed up on his arm and face and neck, but then, he hadn't been that pretty to start with.

"He's gonna pay, man," Trogg said out loud, not so much to Jacker as to the Universe itself. "We're gonna find him and we're going to make him scream and beg to die."

BOLAN SAT AT THE interrogation room table with the rookie, Officer Paglia, opposite him, both of them shuffling through files. The impromptu work space had that entrenched locker-room tang that so many rooms like it never lost—sweat, mostly, mixed with stale air, peeling paint, and the stink of bodies long neglected and abused by their owners. Bolan's credentials had gotten him the space and enough cooperation to get the young officer assigned to him for support, but Syracuse's chief of police and his federal counterparts had made it clear they weren't happy to have him butting in. Bolan didn't care what they thought as long as they stayed out of his way.

"This is everything you have on the Purists and any killings involving them?" Bolan asked.

"Everything—murders we believe or that we know they've committed, and all of the killings of Purist members in the area," Paglia confirmed. He shrugged. "To be honest, a lot of guys on the force seem to think the folks upstairs don't want to try real hard to solve those." He pointed to several crime-scene photos depicting what could only be dead bikers.

Bolan nodded. The Purists were scum and their deaths were no big loss. But innocent victims were getting caught in the cross fire. A vigilante war had been launched, and the killer apparently saw everyone who got in his way as legitimate targets, even if they had nothing to do with the gang or its members.

"What are you looking for?" Paglia asked. Bolan looked up at the young man. There was real intuition there—and Paglia could obviously see that Bolan was no by-the-book, procedural investigator or forensics analyst. The soldier decided to be honest with the cop.

"I need some way to predict where the killer will go next," he admitted. "I can't stay one step behind him. I've got to anticipate his moves so I can cut him off."

Paglia considered the photographs and manila files, then started hunting through them. "I think I know," he said.

Bolan watched, curious.

"Here." Paglia presented him with a file. "As far as I know, there's been no hit there, but the location is central to Purist operations. I've heard rumors through the force that we've tried a couple of times to get under-cover agents in the gang, specifically to get a look at this place. The word is that this is where the bodies are buried."

"And?" Bolan pressed.

"Can't get in." Paglia shrugged. "They're too suspi-cious or just too smart. They won't accept someone they don't know. At least, that's what I've heard."

Bolan considered that. While relatively new to the force, Paglia was typical of police officers every-where—hooked into gossip that was more true than false, though never completely accurate. The thin blue line was shot through with grapevines. You could drop a pen in the break room of a station house at three in the morning and, by five past three, every cop on duty within ten miles would know about it.

In the file photo, an innocuous building sat on a street corner in a vaguely industrial-commercial district. A large, fading sign on the front of the facade pro-claimed it Zippers Arcade.

"You want to find the Purists," Paglia told him, "go to Zippers. If you don't find them first, they'll find *you.*"

Bolan nodded. It was time to make a move.

THE SEEDY BAR AT THE corner of East Fayette Street and Columbus Avenue bore a cracked but still-bright sign proclaiming it Club Lightning. A stylized lightning bolt striking the silhouette of a man and woman adorned the sign and, Rook presumed, invoked its name. Across the street from the bar—which bore several No Loitering notices and boasted a metal sign forbidding the possession of guns, knives and drugs on the premises—was an equally seedy barbershop. Close examination of both buildings would reveal several old bullet holes. The corner of East Fayette and Columbus was notorious in Syracuse. Shootings occurred there regularly, thanks to violence in and around the club. Several attempts to shut down the bar under public safety ordinances had failed.

Rook pulled his pickup truck to a stop in the barbershop's parking lot, blocking the exit. An African-American man in his late teens or early twenties immediately exited the shop and challenged him.

"Hey, man," he said. "You can't park that there. Move your ass."

Without hesitation, Rook shot him.

The .45 ACP round from Rook's four-inch Smith & Wesson 625 Mountain Gun punched through the young man's chest and turned his white shirt a bloody red. Without pausing, Rook walked calmly across the street, drawing his second Smith & Wesson 625 with his left hand. The Hogue grips on both weapons felt warm in his palms. He did not break stride as he kicked in the door, planting his foot in the center of the metal warning sign.

The Whiteshirts were strange bedfellows to the CNY Purists but, as Rook had discovered, drugs and drug money often forged alliances between otherwise bitter enemies. An inner-city gang composed primarily of young black men, the Whiteshirts' uniform was simple: plain cotton T-shirts, usually worn many sizes too large, sometimes with white bandannas. They were among the city's more brutal gangs.

Rook had known for some time that the CNY Purists used the Whiteshirts to distribute drugs throughout Whiteshirt territory. The white supremacist philosophy of the Purists did not seem to get in the way of using an allegedly inferior race to extend their reach and their profits. The fact that most of the customers were of the same race as their subcontractor pushers was probably something the Purists thought greatly amusing.

Rook didn't care about most of that. He didn't care about the politics, he didn't care about the socioeconomic impact of crime in the city, and he didn't care who was selling what to whom. That was a job for the police—a job they'd been failing at for some time. For years city leaders had resolutely denied that there *were* gangs operating in Syracuse, despite what everyone knew to be true. Rook could never understand how they thought pretending the problem didn't exist would change reality.

All that mattered to Rook was that hurting the Whiteshirts would hurt the Purists. The more Rook kept up the pressure, the more he hurt them, the easier it would be to hurt them *again.* He would go on hurting them, too, until he'd gotten them all or until he was dead.

Jennifer deserved no less.

The heavy metal door gave under Rook's booted foot, swinging inward on rusted hinges. The interior of the club was dark and smoke filled, some of it cigar and cigarette, some of it pot, all of it illegal in a state that outlawed smoking in all public buildings. Rook almost laughed out loud as he considered administering the death penalty for this particular violation.

He shot the first man he saw. In the darkness, with his pupils contracted from the outside light, he could barely see at all. He targeted shadows and movement, emptying both revolvers in an ear-stinging fusillade. He shot the bartender. He shot a waitress running for the back, where he presumed an exit through the rudimentary kitchen offered faint hope of safety. The revolvers clicked empty and he holstered them. Switching to his 1911s, he hammered slugs through furniture and people. There was no resistance and no shots were fired at him.

It had been a slaughter.

As his eyes adjusted to the dim light, Rook counted a pair of Whiteshirts near the door and three more sprawled on the floor by the bar. The other bodies were collateral damage. Rook dismissed them. Anyone in the club was up to no good, regardless of their connection—or lack of it—to the Purists.

Rook spun on his heel and made for the door. He knew he'd have to move fast. The cops were never far from this part of town. He needed to be a long way away before they arrived on the scene. In the meantime, another message—and another declaration of war— had been left for the Purists, courtesy of their hired help.

PICK MCWILLIAMS, dressed in a gold shirt and khaki pants in an attempt to blend with the crowd, sat in the airport bar nursing a beer. He glanced around nervously and checked his watch again. He'd checked the boards. The man Trogg had called "Kohler's guest" was late because his flight had been delayed. McWilliams had been waiting for almost two hours and was getting stiff and sore.

McWilliams was trying in vain to signal the bartender from his booth for another beer when he saw the man enter the lounge. McWilliams had no physical description to go by, but this newcomer had to be the right guy. His eyes never stopped moving. He watched every corner of the bar almost at once as he stalked through it like he wanted to kill everyone. If what Trogg had said about Kohler's brief phone call was true, the guy *could* kill everyone there, McWilliams thought.

The newcomer zeroed in on McWilliams almost immediately, his eyes narrowing as he took in the biker's out-of-date clothing. He made his way to the booth and sat without invitation, his hands hidden beneath the table.

"Well. Aren't you a piece of work," he said. His voice was smooth, deep and quiet. It was the voice of a man who didn't shout, who didn't repeat himself. It was the voice of a man who was used to getting what he wanted the first time he asked.

"Pick," McWilliams said, extending a hand. The man's gaze flickered to it disdainfully before centering on his face. McWilliams withdrew his hand, feeling like a sucker, and swallowed his pride. Getting angry with this dangerous bastard would only get his ticket punched.

"Carleton," the man said.

McWilliams didn't know if it was a first name or a last name. He did not ask. Carleton was maybe five-nine, five-ten, and nearly two hundred pounds. His hair was cropped close; his face was outlined by a severely trimmed mustache and beard. He was wearing a black button-down silk shirt, a subdued black-and-gray tie and black slacks under an expensive looking trench coat that might have been Armani. McWilliams didn't know if Armani made coats, but he knew money when he saw it. This Carleton did well for himself and had a big Rolex watch on his wrist to show for it.

"I was told someone would meet me," Carleton said.

McWilliams said nothing. He produced a large manila envelope and slid it across the table.

"Next time," Carleton said with a sigh, "slide it *under* the table." He opened the folder while holding it out of sight between his body and the wall against which the booth was set. Looking up at McWilliams from behind small, round, wire-frame glasses, his gaze flickered left and right before coming to rest on the biker again. He said nothing.

"What?" McWilliams finally asked.

"I was just thinking that Kohler strikes me as a lot more professional than, well, you," he said. "What's a worm like you doing in his employ?"

"I don't work for him," McWilliams said. "I'm with the Purists."

"I'm sure you are," Carleton said, waving one black-gloved hand. His tone was clear. He didn't know or care who or what the Purists might be. "Regardless, when Kohler contacted me he said he had a serious problem. If I had a *serious* problem, I would hardly send the likes of you to convey it."

"Now just wait a minute," McWilliams began, finding his nerve. "Just who the hell do you—"

Something jabbed him.

"Ow!" McWilliams jumped in his seat. "What did you just do?"

"Mr. Pick," Carleton said, cutting off the biker before McWilliams could protest, "have you heard the expression 'shoot the messenger'?"

McWilliams started to go for the revolver in the back of his waistband, but his arms suddenly felt heavy and warm. He kept trying to reach for the gun, but his limbs wouldn't obey. His head felt wobbly as he looked at Carleton, confused.

Carleton smiled tightly. "Thank you for the information. Good day."

McWilliams could only watch as his visitor stood and strode out of the bar, the envelope in one hand. As the well-dressed man swept past a trash can at the entrance, he dropped something in it. McWilliams caught a glimpse of what he thought was a syringe.

He was already slumping in his chair, his throat closing, his breath catching as he tried and failed to cry out. He struggled to draw air, feeling and hearing the croak that left his lips.

Eventually, someone in the bar noticed him sitting there, flailing, and rushed over to try the Heimlich maneuver. By then it was far too late. Pick McWilliams was dead of anaphylactic shock before the EMTs were even called.

ZIPPERS ARCADE WAS A strip club sprawled in a commercial-industrial area on the northern fringes of Syracuse, with an auto yard on one side and a custom upholstery shop on the other. The Executioner had contacted Barbara Price to cross-reference the local data Paglia had provided. Given the size of the city and the scope of the operation—neither of which was particularly significant in the grand scheme of things—there wasn't much, but Aaron Kurtzman had managed to turn up a few morsels.

The upholstery place, a family business in Syracuse founded forty years previously, was legitimate. The auto yard wasn't. Tracing its ownership and the ownership of Zippers produced a common front company that was itself a placeholder for a trust that owned multiple other properties. Most of those properties had been connected to Purist-related violence. The trail went all the way back to something called the Diamond Corporation, headed by one Roger Kohler.

Kohler would receive Bolan's attention in due time. For the moment, the soldier needed to find whoever was killing the Purists—and anyone else who stumbled into the path of the killer's bullets.

Bolan left his SUV parked nearby, in the parking lot of a closed service station. Its windows were boarded over and bore faded paper signs proclaiming For Sale or Lease. He circled to the rear of the block of businesses and walked casually through the neighboring lot behind them. A dark, three-quarter-length windbreaker worn over his blacksuit covered his hardware from casual observers. Nothing in his manner was furtive or otherwise suspicious. He walked as if he belonged there, at a brisk but unhurried pace. He saw a few pedestrians. Traffic was moderate. It consisted mostly of delivery trucks, most likely headed to the assembly warehouse and lumberyard visible in the distance.

The back door of Zippers was labeled and unmanned. Bolan spotted a closed-circuit television camera aimed in his direction and paused. He looked hard at the device, then resumed his course. Up close, he confirmed what he'd thought to be the case—the cable leading from the rear of the camera terminated directly against a four-by-four wooden post set in the asphalt overlooking the rear of the club. It was a good bet nobody had taken the time to hollow out the post in order to run a cable down its length. The device was a dummy, the kind anyone could buy from a novelty catalog. As he approached he noticed the generic warning sticker pasted to the back door, claiming the building was protected by an alarm system.

Reaching out with his left hand, his right inside the windbreaker, Bolan tried the door handle.

The metal fire door swung silently open.

"Gotcha!" yelled the Purist in biker leathers and colors who stood just on the other side of the door. The twin muzzles of the sawed-off double-barrel shotgun in his fists looked very large as Bolan stared down their bores. He heard the metallic clicks of the weapon's twin hammers being cocked.

"Wait—" Bolan said.

The roar of the shotgun was deafening at close range.

4

Bolan folded his knees beneath him as he spoke, dropping down and back in a controlled fall. The shotgun blast washed over him—he could feel the heat on his face. As he landed on his back, his chin tucked in to protect his head, he lashed out with a vicious kick that caught the gunman at the ankle.

Bone snapped. The man dropped like a felled tree, screaming. He'd spent both barrels in the shotgun. Bolan was up and on top of him before he could maneuver to reload. The Executioner drew his Beretta 93-R from its custom shoulder holster. The sound suppressore was already affixed, and three flat slaps signaled the biker's end.

Ears ringing from the close-range shotgun blast, Bolan bent to pick up the fallen weapon. He dropped it into a nearby trash can, where it wouldn't be quickly found and used against him. Then the soldier stepped over the corpse and made his way cautiously through the door, leading with the Beretta. He had lost the element of surprise with that 12-gauge detonation. He would have to rely on simple, brutal force. He shrugged out of his windbreaker and let it drop, giving him un-obstructed access to his combat harness and gear.

The corridor was empty. Bolan's combat boots were loud on the creaking floorboards. He stopped, listened. There was no sign that anyone within had heard the shotgun, which made no sense.

He was staring down a dirty, poorly lit corridor lined in old wood paneling and cluttered with piles of old newspapers and a couple of stinking plastic bags of trash. The corridor terminated in a T leading left and right. Tattered posters for X-rated movies papered the far wall. From somewhere ahead came the muffled bass of dance music, obviously from the main area of the club. Bolan took another step and the floor creaked again. He froze.

He heard the answering creak from around the corner.

They were waiting for him, playing it smart, they thought. Bolan quietly plucked a flash-bang grenade from his combat harness. He triggered the little hockey-puck shaped device—one of Kissinger's little helpers, as Cowboy called them—and threw it at an angle so it bounced off the far wall and ricocheted around the corner. Quickly he crouched, turned away, and shoved his hands over his ears while opening his mouth wide and squeezing his eyes shut. The deafening, blinding eruption was mercifully brief, so bright he could see the flash through his closed eyes.

Bolan was up and stalking as the afterimages of the blast left floating green shapes in his vision. There were three of them writhing on the floor—two to the right and one to the left, where they'd been waiting to ambush him. Two handguns and a shotgun littered the floor. The men wore Purist colors. This time he didn't bother collecting weapons; he simply moved on, reloading the Beretta to replace the partially spent magazine with a fresh twenty rounds.

He chose the right-hand corridor; the left was a dead end that terminated in a bare cinder-block wall. Bolan made his way down the hallway, keeping his head, arms and weapon steady and searching for adversaries. There was a shriek, and then another. Ahead of him, he saw movement. Suddenly, five half-naked women ran from a dressing room ahead and to the left, brushing past him as if he wasn't even there. Bolan let the strippers pass, his Beretta held at low ready. He waited.

The two gunners ducked out, one high, one low. The bottom man got off a shot that went high and wide. Bolan drilled him with two bursts through the torso, the Beretta rising to sweep the top man in the same arc. The second man—both were dressed in Zippers T-shirts and khakis, probably what passed for club security in this crime pit—was punched backward as the slugs entered his neck and chin. The little .380 Colt Mustang he had been clutching fell from nerveless fingers and clattered on the floor.

Bolan took the corner wide to maximize his cover and keep any potential targets in his field of vision as he entered the dressing room. He passed the lighted mirrors and scattered lingerie without a glance, instead scanning every corner for hidden threats. The door leading from the dressing room to the main part of the club was shut. He planted one boot just left of the doorknob and cracked it open without trying the handle, diving low as he entered.

"Now! Now!" someone yelled. Gunfire ripped from three points at once and Bolan had no choice but to blitz forward, legs pumping. The club area was multileveled, colored lights washing down from scaffolding on the ceiling. One of the shooters was in the DJ booth, where deafening techno continued to bleat from mammoth speakers along the walls. Another was somewhere in the scaffolding—Bolan couldn't tell where—and a third was on the move on the lower dance-floor level. Bullets ripped the slick tiling behind Bolan's feet as he ran for the DJ booth. Strobe lights flashed from above, obscuring the muzzle-flashes from the gang members' guns. There were no customers. Bolan had reached the club before it opened. With the strippers gone, he knew chances were good there no innocents to get caught in the cross fire.

With no cover afforded by the tiered but largely open club area, Bolan shoved the Beretta before him and unleashed a fusillade of 9 mm rounds at the DJ booth, forcing the gunman there to duck. Gunfire followed him as the other two shooters tried to claim him, but he was moving too fast and the colored, flashing lights were causing the Purists as much trouble as they were causing the soldier. Bolan threw himself flat beside the half-height doorway to the DJ booth. The biker within—a broken, older-looking man with a shaved head, wearing a leather jacket with one sleeve cut off— swung his short-barreled 9 mm Colt submachine gun in Bolan's direction, but he was too slow. The Exectutioner stitched him up the groin and through the torso, emptying the Beretta with two last triple bursts.

The two remaining shooters concentrated their fire on Bolan's position. He stayed low, letting them rip up the wall above his head, dousing him with drywall dust. The dead Purist had several spare magazines for his Colt, so Bolan appropriated them and the weapon, shoving the long stick magazines under his web belt at his side. He reloaded his Beretta and holstered it, then reached up blindly and began slapping buttons on the DJ board. On the fourth try, the music stopped. Bolan slapped a couple of more buttons and managed to switch off the strobe lights and the track lighting, plunging Zippers into darkness.

He waited for the shooting to stop, then crept silently from the booth, feeling his way along the outer wall of the club area, walking in a low crouch with a corner of the Colt's telescoping stock tucked against his shoulder. Then he stopped and remained perfectly still, controlling his breathing.

"Gord!" one of the Purists finally shouted. "Gord! Gordy, man, where are you?"

"Over here, moron," Gordy finally answered.

"Do you see him?"

"No, Chigger, I don't see him. If I saw him, I'd be shooting at him! I can't see anything."

"I don't hear him."

There was a pause. Bolan waited. He very quietly slipped the combat light from his pocket and held it in his fingers, wrapping his remaining free support-hand fingers around the forestock of the Colt.

"I think he snuck out!" Chigger offered from a spot across the room and to Bolan's right. "Maybe when the lights were out!"

"Damn it," Gordy said from his position in the scaffolding. "Trogg's going to have our asses."

Bolan aimed his Colt into the scaffolding and triggered the combat light. The blinding beam painted Gordy in stark relief against the scaffold struts. He squinted and flinched, bringing a hand up in front of his face, just as Bolan sprayed him with three controlled bursts. Gordy didn't even scream as he fell to the dance floor in a heap.

Chigger began firing, his weapon cracking with the distinct hollow sound of an AK variant. But Bolan had moved while dousing his light, leaving only an afterimage in Chigger's already crippled night vision. The gang member was still firing several yards to Bolan's right as the soldier flanked him. When the Executioner triggered the light again, Chigger was too busy emptying his 30-round magazine into the shadows to react. Bolan pumped a stream of Parabellum rounds into his legs, toppling him. The submachine gun clattered to the floor.

Bolan walked up to Chigger, keeping the light on the biker's face. Chigger squinted through the pain and turned away, grabbing at his bloody legs. One of his knees was almost completely gone. A pool of blood spread rapidly beneath him.

"You'll be a long time bleeding out that way," Bolan told him flatly. "Tell me how you knew I was coming."

"You're him," Chigger managed weakly. "You bastard..."

"What are you talking about?" Bolan nudged the fading man with one boot.

"You're the guy who's been...been killing Purists... killing my brothers, man."

Bolan frowned. "How did you know I was coming?" he asked.

Chigger gestured weakly toward the direction Bolan had come. "Office," he said quietly before losing consciousness.

Bolan wasted no time backtracking, finding the office door just off the entrance to the club proper. Covering the door with the Colt, he entered quickly and found the room deserted. It was a mess, a clutter of trash, empty beer bottles and the detritus of a poorly kept office. In one corner of the single, disorganized desk, a combination copier-fax-telephone sat idle. A single fax sat in its paper tray. Bolan picked it up and read it.

This probe was a bust. The fax contained a description of Bolan. The Purists thought he was the vigilante. Out of leads, he would have to go back and start again. It was possible Paglia could point him to a secondary location.

He left the lights off as he exited. Zippers was out of business, at least for now.

ROOK'S PICKUP TRUCK rolled to a stop on abused brakes. He opened the grime-filmed automatic passenger window for a better view—only to see the commando marching from the front entrance. There he was, as big as life, wearing full combat harness and covered in gear and grenades.

The man in black stopped just long enough to eyeball Rook.

Rook stared back, then floored the accelerator, ducking forward as he sent his truck tearing down Teall Avenue with all the tire squealing its low-end torque could muster.

The chase was on.

BOLAN RAN FOR HIS SUV, vaulting a chain-link fence separating the adjacent parking lot as he did so. He made it to the truck, fired it up and roared straight through the fence, pouring it on to make up speed. The twisted fencing behind him rattled and squealed as a portion caught on his rear bumper and was then pulled free. Bolan ignored it. He caught a break as he saw the big pickup truck fishtailing through an intersection ahead. He cut to the right and took a side street, then cut over, thundering around the curve. Horns blared as offended or frightened drivers scrambled to get out of the way. His SUV had more speed than the vigilante's, however. It was only a few blocks before he was right behind the truck, swerving and dodging as he stuck to the other man's trail through the narrow streets.

ROOK KEPT ONE EYE ON the rearview mirror and one on the traffic before him, swerving madly as he careered through an intersection and ran several sets of red lights in the process. Behind him, tires squealed and metal crunched as a couple of drivers collided. Rook barely noticed them. He was too focused on the man in black in the SUV close behind.

Unlimbering one of his 1911s, Rook thumbed off the slide safety and used the butt of the gun to hit the window release on his side. Cocking his left arm upside down, pointing his elbow forward, he started firing blindly behind him, wincing at the .45 ACP detonations so close to his left ear. He'd have some ringing and maybe even some partial hearing loss for a time. It didn't matter. Rook knew only that he had to get away. If he faced the commando, there was no telling what would happen—which might mean his work would be cut short. He would not let that happen. Not for Jennifer. Not for him.

Rook did not notice when one of his rounds caught an elderly woman exiting a drug store as the truck bulled past. He kept firing until the magazine was empty, cursing as he worked the slide release with his left index finger and shoved the empty gun back into his shoulder holster. Drawing awkwardly with his left arm, he managed to unleather the identical .45 and bring it into action. As he did so, he almost hit a minivan that cut across his path from a side street. Holding his breath, he managed to avoid the collision. Before he knew it the truck was almost airborne as it shot up and over a hill leading to the end of Grant Boulevard. The big truck caromed off, then bounced over the curb as Rook struggled to keep control, throwing the vehicle into a wide slide that brought him to the entrance to the city's minor league baseball stadium. He took the curve, bouncing up over the concrete gutters, burning rubber as he floored it through a series of switchbacks that would take him past the Regional Transportation Center and toward the monster shopping mall on the shores of Onondaga Lake. A mall meant people, and people meant cover. If he couldn't lose the commando in the mall traffic, he'd see how the big bastard liked trying to take a shot at Rook through a crowded shopping mall.

It was then that Rook heard the sirens.

The City of Syracuse black-and-whites surged up from Park Street and blocked the intersection leading to the mall. Rook could see the officers exiting their vehicles and bringing shotguns to bear. Before they could fire, he took the cruiser on the right, clipping its front fender as he cut right onto Park Street. The SUV followed, scraping the police car with the left rear fender of the Blazer. Rook took them onto Onondaga Lake Parkway, standing on the accelerator and pushing his pickup for all it was worth. The SUV stayed tight to his tail.

Rook was running out of room. He cursed. The parkway terminated at a busy intersection. There was little chance he could get through without a collision, not at his speed. The commando was right on his tail.

Suddenly he had a plan.

He ripped the steering wheel to the left, powering through a tight turn that brought him tearing through the entrance to Onondaga Lake Park. The skate park and children's playground lay just beyond. Several small children were playing on the brightly colored equipment.

Rook rammed the metal barrier blocking the asphalt drive leading to the park and its adjacent walking trail.

He brought the truck to a stop next to the playground. Jumping from the cab, he ran for the nearest knot of children.

BOLAN'S SUV SQUEALED TO a stop on smoking tires, veering around the truck and blocking its nose. Behind him, sirens wailing, the Syracuse police blocked the exit with their own cruisers. Bolan knew they'd treat him as a threat just as readily as they would the vigilante, but it didn't matter. By the time they got to sorting everything out, it wouldn't matter.

"No!" Bolan shouted.

The vigilante scooped up a young girl, pistol-whipping the woman with her. The woman dropped and the little girl, perhaps three years old, began screaming and struggling. Her captor ignored her, tucking her under his arm as if she weighed nothing. He brought the big revolver—Bolan saw one like it on the man's belt— to her temple and cocked the hammer.

"Stop right there," the vigilante growled. Bolan had drawn his Desert Eagle and kept the triangular muzzle leveled at the man's head.

"Don't try," the vigilante said, smirking. "Shoot me in the face and I'll still pull this trigger and splatter her all over both of us."

"Let her go," Bolan said.

"No," the vigilante said.

"Put your weapons down!" the two police officers ordered. One carried his riot gun and another had a de-partment-issue Smith & Wesson pistol trained on first the vigilante, then Bolan, then back again to the vigilante.

"I'm with the Justice Department," Bolan announced, as much for the vigilante's benefit as for the police. "Contact Office Paglia. He'll confirm it."

"I said drop your weapons!" one of the cops commanded.

The vigilante's eyes narrowed.

"Don't!" Bolan cautioned. He extended his support hand and lowered the Desert Eagle. "Look, she's innocent. Let her go and you can walk. Don't make it worse."

The vigilante's face softened. The revolver's four-inch barrel moved away from the little girl...and toward Bolan.

"Too bad," the vigilante said. "For you."

With that, he pumped four rounds into Bolan's chest.

5

Kohler lay prone on the weight bench. He was drenched in sweat, feeling the sweet burn through his chest and arms, the feeling of an hour well spent in his private gym. Above him, his bodyguard, Abbot, stood by, silent, impassive. If Kohler hadn't known better, he would think the thick-necked fireplug of a man, his scalp shining under his severe crew cut, wasn't paying attention. Nothing got past Abbot, however. If Kohler showed even the slightest hint of losing the bar during the press, Abbot would be there to place it back in its brackets. If anyone approached Kohler on the street with so much as an unkind glance, Kohler had only to snap his fingers before Abbot stomped them flat. The bodyguard was also a decent sparring partner, though he was slower than Kohler and did not provide enough of a challenge. Still, he stood in for Kohler's regular victims when no one else was available. Kohler did not like to use him for that too much. Abbot was too useful to put out of commission with broken ribs or some other injury, the "accidents" that befell his sparring opponents only too regularly.

Kohler concentrated, pushing the bar up off the bench and slowly, smoothly pushing out a series of repetitions, the bar and its impressive stack of weights growing heavier with each press. Kohler replaced the bar, counted off thirty seconds, and did another set. Arms trembling slightly, he replaced the bar in its bracket as Abbot looked on, the burly man never moving so much as an inch.

Kohler eased himself up and Abbot immediately placed a monogrammed towel in his employer's hand, unasked. Kohler began toweling off the sweat when the slim telephone on Abbot's belt began to ring.

Still silent, Abbot glanced to Kohler, who closed his eyes for a long moment and then nodded. Abbot snapped the phone open and placed it to Kohler's ear. Kohler did not open his eyes and did not take the phone. He said nothing.

"I'm here," the lilting voice said from the other end. "It's the strangest thing. Apparently, Mr. McWilliams was deathly allergic to peanut oil."

"I've no idea to whom you are referring," Kohler said smoothly, "but I've heard such things can happen. You received the package?"

"I did," Carleton confirmed. "There's not much to go on."

"There will be," Kohler told him. "I've got people on it now. Make whatever arrangements you usually make and wait for a call. Then do what you've been paid to do."

"Yes, about that."

"Yes?"

"My people tell me only half the fee has been transferred."

"Yes."

"That was not the agreement."

Kohler's back went rigid. He opened his eyes and snatched the phone from Abbot's hand. "You listen to me," he said evenly. "You will receive the remaining half on completion. I do not pay up front in full. I never have and I never will. I'm not one of the spineless desk jockeys you're used to dealing with, either. Fuck with me and I'll see to it that you never *work* again."

"I understand," Carleton said.

"Good. I'd prefer to keep this professional."

"Fair enough," Carleton acknowledged. He ended the call without another word.

Kohler snapped the phone shut and handed it absently to Abbot. One problem out of the way and another one soon to be solved.

There were times, he had to admit, when his line of work was positively *tiresome*.

"Abbot," he said, "bring the car around for later. We'll need it when I've finished with my other obligations today. We've an appointment to keep."

TROGG, WITH JACKER IN TOW at Club Lightning, faced what was left of the Purists. Segregating themselves to one side were the Whiteshirts, who stood in a surly knot. Their losses over the past few days had been severe and both groups were reeling.

From within his cluster of supporters, H-Dog, leader of the Whiteshirts, was posturing and throwing gang signs, saying something too quiet for the Purists to hear. He was a monster of a man, almost as big as Trogg, but his body was much more defined—the result of hours spent working out in prison yards. He was covered in crude, dark, jailhouse tattoos.

"What I got here," Trogg told the assembled gang members, "is the last of our straps and all the ammo we could pile together. We got handguns, we got AKs, we got some Uzis. We got one rocket launcher and three rockets—" he gestured to the Russian-made RPG on the table "—and we got *balls*."

The barroom was thick with smoke and smelled of sweat, urine and fear. Trogg looked around the dim area and pointed a thick finger at the Whiteshirts. "What about you?" he demanded. "You got the balls to do what needs to be done?"

"Man," H-Dog said quietly, "I am sick to death of hearin' 'bout your balls, man. Make your case or shut the hell up."

Trogg snorted. "Look," he said, sweeping a brawny arm across the room. "This guy, he's hit us and hit us. He don't care who he kills. He's on some kinda mission, right? Well, we can go nuts looking for him. We can try to catch him at his own game—but Chigger, Gordy, Smitty, Trey and Steve, not to mention a couple other guys, already found out that won't work. We can run and hide—" this was greeted with jeers from around the room "—or we can make him play *our* game. The Boss called me early this morning. We've got help on the way. All we have to do is set this up right and we can take the guy who's been chewing on us, take him all the way to the morgue."

"Get to the point," H-Dog demanded. "What are we going to do?"

"First, you're all gonna look at these," Trogg said, waving around a rumpled copy of the sketch Jacker had made. "Then, we're gonna gear up. And we're going to do something that nobody, not this asshole, not the cops, not anybody, can ignore. And we're gonna get paid big-time for it."

Camillus, New York

BOLAN FROWNED INTO THE scrambled satellite phone. "Are you sure he's reliable, Hal?"

"Positive," Brognola said. "Larry Kearney was the scourge of the Potomac before the powers that be encouraged him to move north. He's a character, but he's the most brutally honest person I know—and he's a real pit bull when he thinks he's got a story. From the sounds of things, you're at a dead end. Larry can set you right. If anyone knows that town, it's Larry. I'm betting he has the place wired."

"Let's hope so," Bolan said. "Have you got Bear working on the composite sketch I sent to you?"

"He's processing it now," Brognola acknowledged. "I've also gotten a lot more from the Syracuse police than your suspect's likeness. They're raising holy Hell about your 'strong-arm tactics,' as they put it."

"Stall them for me," Bolan said. "I'll try to steer clear of them. I can't afford to get tangled up in any more red tape." He closed the phone and replaced it in a slit pocket of his blacksuit, checking the fit of the three-quarter-length coat he wore to conceal his hardware. It was a little heavier than he'd prefer, but not too bad in the cool air. His windbreaker was somewhere at Zippers, and he would not be going back for it.

Bolan exited the SUV and took a look around the neighborhood.

His chest still ached where his Second Chance vest, worn beneath his blacksuit, had absorbed the vigilante's slugs. The impacts had been enough to knock him flat. He'd been forced to watch with the police as the vigilante took the little girl with him, warning them not to follow or he'd kill the hostage. Against Bolan's recommendations the police had given in to the man's demands. He had disappeared. The good news was that the girl had been found shortly thereafter, at a convenience store where her kidnapper had dumped her. She was shaken up but otherwise unharmed.

The little house in Camillus, a western suburb of Syracuse, sat in a development of similar homes. While it was unremarkable from the outside, Bolan quickly noticed the surveillance cameras mounted in the front yard and overlooking the front door. The window glass of the house was reflective, as if coated for one-way viewing. The front door itself was painted steel, not wood. There was a house number and a mailbox, but no name on or below either. The single-car garage boasted another surveillance camera. Its door was shut and its windows had been boarded and painted to match the door itself.

Bolan approached and stood before the front door. An unmarked doorbell, painted to blend with the wall, was the only option. He pressed it and waited. When there was no response, he pressed it again.

"What? What the hell do you want?" a voice drawled.

"Mr. Kearney?" Bolan asked, looking around. He could not see the concealed speaker from which the voice emitted. He assumed the connection was two-way.

"Who-all wants to know?" the voice drawled back.

"My name is Cooper," Bolan said. "Hal Brognola sent me."

"Brognola?" the voice came back. "Hell, son, why didn't you say so?"

There was a mechanical buzzing noise and the steel door released on automatic bolts. Bolan pushed it cautiously aside and stepped through.

All three hundred pounds of Larry Kearney waited for him on an easy chair next to a computer desk in the living room. Two flat-screen monitors were connected to a state-of-the-art PC humming quietly on the floor. There was also a smaller monitor split into four screens, obviously the closed-circuit television feeds. It was mounted above a control board governing the house's automated security systems and door locks.

The house was cluttered and lived in, but by no means slovenly. Every wall was covered with bracket-and-board bookshelves, every shelf groaning under the weight of books. These ranged from novels to reference books to stacks of newspapers and clippings. Cardboard dividers were inserted into these at intervals, marking groupings by subject or flagging items of particular interest.

Kearney looked Bolan over from his overstuffed chair. He was holding a Glock 17 on the soldier.

"Howdy," he said.

"Hello," Bolan said, keeping his hands by his sides.

Kearney was middle-aged or older, with a salt-and-pepper beard and a full head of graying hair. Bolan noted the Charles Davis combat cane—a grooved, lacquered affair with a pointed crook—resting against the chair and raised his estimation of Kearney accordingly.

"How do I know Hal really sent you?" Kearney drawled, seeming unconcerned over the issue.

"You don't, really," Bolan shrugged. "But you could call him."

"I could." Kearney shrugged. "But then, I'm the one who asked him to send somebody in the first place." He replaced the Glock in the custom leather shoulder holster he wore, grabbed his cane and levered himself up. He moved slowly but deliberately, as if it pained him but he was determined to ignore it. His dark eyes were sharp nonetheless and his grip very firm when he shook Bolan's hand. "Larry Kearney."

"Cooper," Bolan repeated.

"Sure, if that's what you want to use." Kearney chuckled. He hobbled through the room and out to the adjoining kitchen. "Join me in here," he called over his shoulder. "I've got a pot of coffee on."

Bolan followed to find Kearney pouring coffee into two extralarge mugs. The wooden pedestal table in the small kitchen had matching chairs and was tastefully integrated with the cabinets and other decor in the room. Dirty dishes were stacked with almost obsessive-compulsive orderliness in the sink.

"Forgive the security," Kearney said with a shrug,

making his Glock jiggle in its holster, "but I got to be careful. I've made more than a few enemies over the years, and I wouldn't put it past any of them to show up at my door."

Bolan looked back to where the steel front door was visible through the living room. A Mossberg 590 Mariner, complete with a sidesaddle full of shells and an underbarrel flashlight, was clipped to steel brackets mounted directly to the drywall beside the door. "Something tells me you've got it covered."

"Not always," Kearney said. "I got complacent a couple years back. Was in the grocery store with nothing but my cane and a folding knife, when the old lady of one of my victims walked up to me and about slapped my face off. She'd have knocked me out if I hadn't pulled on her. Didn't have to stick her, though."

"Victims?" Bolan asked.

"I'm a journalist, son," Kearney said. "My job is making people's lives difficult. Back in Wonderland I put all kinds of corrupt politicians in hot water, jail or both. Covered my share of drug houses in West Virginia and Virginia, too. That's how I got the cane."

"How do you mean?"

"I was taking pictures of a chop shop in West Virginia when one of the miscreants caught me at it."

"He shot you?" Bolan asked.

"Nope," Kearney said. "Ran me over with a 1999 Chevy Lumina. Damnedest thing, getting run over. I don't recommend it. Broke my back, can you believe it? One of the quacks I talked to said I would never walk again. Shows what he knows. The average doctor knows as much as the average Associated Press stringer."

Bolan laughed despite himself.

"I have to laugh," Kearney said, "'cause if I didn't, I'd remember just how damned much it hurts. Still, I look at it this way. I'm up and around today. That Lumina? Totaled. That means I won the fight," he said, laughing. "So. What can I do to help the mysterious friend of my friend, Hal Brognola?"

"I'm investigating the CNY Purists," Bolan said. "More specifically, I'm trying to find the man waging war on them."

"Oh," Kearney nodded. "That."

Kearney sipped from his coffee mug then grabbed his cane. "Come on," he drawled. "We'll need the computer. Drag a chair with you."

HALF AN HOUR LATER, Kearney was wrapping up his tour through his files. He had saved the best for last. "This," he said with a flourish, pointing to the screen with one large hand, "is my primary suspect." Over the open files illustrating the Purist hierarchy, virtual news clippings and scanned photos depicting past crime scenes, and links to online news sites, a photo window popped up. A familiar face appeared.

"That's him," Bolan said.

"My bet is that Hal's people—whoever those mysterious folks might be—will confirm this for you," Kearney said, "but I've been tracking this guy for a while now, and I think the puzzle pieces are finally coming together. His daughter died in Saint Joseph's, one of the local hospitals. I did some checking—she was a classic crank case. Crystal meth, and bad. Her dad, one Gary Rook, did not take well to her passing. From everything I've pieced together, he's got the right sort of résumé, too."

"Which is?"

"He was a Marine," Kearney said, "saw combat in Grenada, such as it was. Got out, did some work as a stuntman in Hollywood and New York, if you can believe it, before settling down in this area and taking work at the Carrier plant. Factory work, making air conditioners. Got laid off in the inevitable downsizing a few years ago. Divorced not long after that. Wife went back to Los Angeles, or thereabouts, and was killed in an automobile accident. The daughter, Jennifer Rook, was his only surviving relative."

"So he's a combat veteran," Bolan said. "Knows weaponry. Probably did some other training in the intervening years, maybe martial arts for the camera. He's highly motivated and he's bitter."

"Yep," Kearney confirmed. "And he has nothing to lose."

"A dangerous combination," Bolan nodded. "I have to stop him before anyone else gets hurt."

"He doesn't seem to give a damn who gets in the way, does he?" Kearney asked. "I've done a series of articles on this bastard in the *Hard Times,* my alternative paper hereabouts," he said. "Of course, in a lot of cases, the victims were street scum—members of the CNY Purists or those who run with or traffic for them. My editorial policy, as they say, was to run a few cartoons talking about how great it was that those folks were roasting in hell."

Bolan raised an eyebrow.

"Oh, they didn't like that one bit," Kearney said. "Started sending death threats. Even got what we thought was a human finger in the mail. Turned out to be fake."

"What was it?"

"You don't want to know," Kearney dismissed the matter. "Anyway, I'm convinced this is the guy. Gary Rook, our neighborhood vigilante, working hard to earn the title 'mass murderer.'"

"I've tried to get ahead of this Rook," Bolan said. "I almost had him."

"So I heard over the scanner." Kearney frowned. "Shame about Zippers."

"Why?" Bolan asked. "Were you a customer?"

"No, I mean it's a shame you didn't burn it to the ground. I mean, that *was* your work, wasn't it?"

Bolan said nothing.

"I thought so." Kearney grinned. "Well, the only way to anticipate this guy is to figure out where he might go, what he might hit. I assume you were trying to do that with Zippers. We're going to have to go deeper, find the less obvious hiding spots. I have some material here, but the bulk of my files are at my office at the *Hard Times*. You got a car?"

"You saw it through your cameras, I would think," Bolan said.

"I did, I did." Kearney laughed. "Sorry. Old habits. Let's go."

GARY ROOK SAT cross-legged on the floor of his bedroom. With some difficulty he managed to press down the retaining ring on the foreguard of the Olympic Arms CAR-15 carbine far enough to release the two halves of the guard. These he tossed aside and, with some difficulty as he worked against the spring-loaded ring, worked two new grooved foreguard halves in place. When those were secured he took the other accessories from the cardboard box at his feet, lining up a vertical foregrip and installing a flashlight and mount before it, at the six-o'clock position. The carbine already had a telescoping stock; he had purchased the weapon with a short barrel and a flash-hider that he'd removed, which meant the weapon was shorter than legal by federal law. He laughed mirthlessly at that.

The mil-spec 5.56 mm ammo in large metal cans by his bed had been purchased at a gun show in a neighboring county. He got to work loading 30-round magazines—magazines illegally imported into New York, which still had laughable assault weapon legislation in place. He taped the magazines together in pairs, one up, one down, "jungle clip" style. When he had filled them all, he dropped them in a canvas messenger bag already bulging with ammunition, pistol magazines and revolver moon clips, and other implements of mayhem. He slung the bag over his shoulder, where it hung across his body at his left hip. Shouldering the carbine, he prepared to leave.

He cast one last glance around the apartment.

He would not be back. It was time to settle things, and permanently. He would stay in the truck, on the road, on the prowl, until he tracked down the last of the Purists and put them down.

For you, Jennifer, he thought.

Once in his truck, Rook drove aimlessly. He would have to switch vehicles soon. There were times when he almost wanted to get caught, however. There we times when he almost fantasized about how it would feel when the cops caught up to him, when bullets ripped into his body and sent him to be with Jennifer, forever.

Before he realized it, his truck had taken him to the south side. That was bad because the area was heavily patrolled. The poorest section of the city, it was crime-ridden and miserable.

The south side was full of gangs. Many of them were lesser crews, sometimes as few as three or four young men. Many of them were also Whiteshirts, however. As long as Rook was there, he decided to find a knot of them and take them out. He could probably count on a delayed police response. His attacks elsewhere drew remarkably different levels of scrutiny and emergency response depending on the area. Given how often the gang members plugged away at one another, Rook knew chances were he could be long gone before the first police cruiser showed up.

Rook cruised the neighborhood, searching in a grid pattern, city block by city block. He was about to give up and turn back, head north looking for more opportunities to exact his revenge, when he saw them. On the street corner, loitering in front of a convenience store, was a cluster of Whiteshirts, their baggy shirts and white bandannas unmistakable.

Rook took the CAR-15 from the floor. He removed the magazine, checked it to see if the first round had been stripped out of it. Flipping the safety catch to fire, he braced the rifle across his body on the open window frame of the truck door. Driving with his left hand only, his right fist clenched around the grip of his rifle, he gunned the engine while holding down the brake.

One of the Whiteshirts, hearing the truck's powerful engine from down the block, looked up and straight at him.

Rook released the brake. Low-end torque sent the truck burning down the road on its big tires, its trajectory carrying it past the convenience store. As he drove, Rook stroked the trigger of his CAR-15, squeezing shot after shot through the open window. There were at least half a dozen Whiteshirts. Two of them went down, their chests covered with welling bloodstains, as Rook's fire chipped away at the front of the convenience store. Inside the store, the clerk—an elderly man reading the newspaper—caught a round through the torso. He collapsed on the floor, bleeding and gasping.

Rook stopped the truck and exited, holding the CAR-15 in both fists. He clipped the one-point sling to its quick-connect attachment on the telescoping stock, then brought the rifle to his shoulder. The scattered Whiteshirts, kneeling or lying on the concrete steps of the convenience store, realized that they were still under attack. They struggled to meet the threat. One of them pulled a Glock 36 from the waistband of his baggy pants. Another was fishing around in his cavernous pockets, trying to find whatever hideout pistol he'd been carrying.

Two others scrambled into the convenience store and slammed the metal security grate from inside. Rook dismissed them, for the moment.

The Glock shooter raised his pistol in a horizontal grip and banged out three shots in rapid succession. Rook simply watched him do it.

"The problem," he calmly informed the gang member as he brought his CAR-15 on target, "is that when you hold the pistol to the side like that, barely aiming, you're almost guaranteed to shoot to one side of your target, if you get anywhere near it at all." The CAR-15 barked once. A bloody hole blossomed in the Whiteshirt's forehead. He sank to his knees and then fell over sideways, the Glock skittering across the concrete.

The other gangbanger was still hunting for his gun.

"What's the matter, friend?" Rook taunted him. "Did you forget where you put your gun?" With his left hand he pulled the CAR-15 across his body in a retention and transition position, freeing his right hand. As he loomed over his prey, the young man finally found his gun. When he aimed it at Rook, the ex-Marine almost laughed. The nickel-plated Raven .25 pistol was shaking so much he thought the kid might shoot himself before he hit anyone else.

"Give me that." Rook's hand whipped out like a striking snake, snatching the little gun from the stunned Whiteshirt. Allowing his CAR-15 to hang free on its sling, he pulled back the clunky slide of the dirt-cheap weapon. It was loaded, which didn't surprise him, but neither had he taken it for granted. Some of these punks carried weapons for show but had no bullets to fire.

"A lot of people doubt the effectiveness of a round like this," Rook lectured the trembling Whiteshirt. "But me, I figure no matter how small the bullet is, I don't want to be shot with one. Even a single bullet from a .25 automatic can ruin your whole day, did you know that?"

The Whiteshirt goggled at him, eyes bugging from his head.

"Sure, this is pretty anemic, even worse than .22 rimfire," Rook went on, "but if you use enough of them, sure, they're fatal." He fired from the hip, emptying the little popgun into the Whiteshirt's center of mass. He counted six shots before the gun's magazine was empty.

Riddled with bloody .25-caliber holes, the White-shirt—dead on his knees—fell flat on his face.

"You see?" Rook said.

Rook glanced at his wristwatch. No sirens. There had been plenty of gunfire, but he saw no gawkers, no curious onlookers. A few cars passed, some forced to turn wide to avoid the badly parked truck, but no one stopped and no one seemed inclined to get involved themselves.

Rook tossed the spent pistol aside. He marched up the steps to the convenience store and pushed the door. It didn't budge. He tried firing a combat-booted foot into the door just to the side of the frame, but all he got for his front kick was a sore heel. Undeterred, he walked casually back to his truck, detached his rifle from its sling connector and placed it in the truck's cab.

From the rear of the vehicle, he took a length of tow cable, of the type used to pull another vehicle. Connecting one end of the cable to the safety chain holes in his trailer hitch, Rook ran the other end of the cable to the metal security door. The hook on the end of the tow cable slipped through the grates, and Rook secured it by strapping it back on itself.

Whistling, he got back in the truck, gunned the engine and slammed on the accelerator.

The truck easily ripped the security gate free. It clattered to the ground. Rook exited the truck, drawing his twin .45 pistols, and walked carefully up to the gaping doorway.

"Anybody home?" he asked, ducking his head inside.

"Go away!" one of the Whiteshirts called from inside. He had to admit that nobody had actually tried that before—simply telling him to get lost.

"Now, that's just rude," Rook said. He fired a couple of shots into the store.

The answering shotgun blast almost took off his head. Apparently one of the two gang members had found a weapon in the store.

"I'm coming in!" Rook said.

There was another shotgun blast, followed by the unmistakable sound of a shotgun's action being opened. Rook charged inside. He found one of the Whiteshirts just inside the doorway and clubbed him in the face with the butt of his .45. The other was behind the store's counter, struggling to reload a double-barreled shotgun. Rook walked up on him calmly and pointed the .45 at him.

"I'd drop that, if I were you."

The Whiteshirt let his weapon fall heavily to the floor. Rook did not even notice the old man behind the counter or, if he did, he did not connect the man's death to anything meaningful or significant.

"What you rollin' on us for?" the Whiteshirt said.

"Shut up," Rook said. He bashed the kid across the face with the barrel of his gun.

TRACY WILSON SAT BEHIND his desk in the foyer of the *Hard Times* office, wishing he was just about anywhere else. Granted, his was not a difficult job, but easy only took you so far into an eight-hour day. As the security guard and de facto receptionist at the *Hard Times*, he was the first line of defense—and the the only line of defense, unless you counted Larry Kearney himself. The *Hard Times* was well-known as righter than right, what Kearney called "a truly alternative paper in a left-leaning region of already left-leaning New York State."

For his part, Wilson was apolitical. He worked as a security guard for Kearney because Kearney let him carry his pistol. Every once in a while, protestors would picket the office. Now and again one of them would work up the courage to come inside, which meant Wilson had to throw them out or call the cops. He'd never once drawn his gun on the job, nor did he figure he ever would. The protestors and crackpots were usually content with shouting at the building from the street, or maybe flipping him off and shouting at him before they drifted away. Larry Kearney never seemed to notice them, though Wilson secretly wondered if he wasn't plotting to bring in old-time head-breakers to bust up the picket lines when they occurred. Wilson wouldn't put it past him.

The man who entered the building stopped to look from left to right when he closed the door behind him. Wilson looked up and frowned. The newcomer was wearing Purist colors—a denim vest over a leather jacket, worn with tattered blue jeans and engineer's boots—textbook outlaw biker, of the type decried regularly in Kearney's editorials.

As the biker went for a gun in his belt and Wilson, too slowly, thought to draw his own, it was the look in the biker's eyes that told Wilson his life wasn't so boring anymore.

It was a lot shorter.

6

Wearing a hotel robe, Carleton lounged on the end of the king-size bed in his hotel room, watching the large television with only mild interest. In the bathroom, the high-priced escort finished whatever she was doing and emerged, wearing only a thong and high heels. She wore too much makeup, and Carleton had managed to smear most of it in his enthusiasm. Still, she was not bad at all, especially considering the available talent in a nowhere city like Syracuse. Large, firm breasts—likely implants, but he didn't care—a taut belly, shapely legs, a smooth, round bottom; what was not to like? He considered running a tab and taking her again. Before he could suggest it, his cell phone began to chime out a reasonable approximation of Beethoven's Fifth.

He took a wad of bills from the wallet in his slacks, which were draped over a chair by the bed. He tossed the money to the call girl, who caught it. She pulled her dress over her head and left the room without a word.

He snapped open the phone. "Yes?" he asked.

"I have a time and a location coordinated," Kohler told him. "This is important. I have attended to it personally. Do not fail."

"I never do," Carleton said confidently. "That's why you hired me and not someone else, remember?"

"Just get it done," Kohler said, and hung up.

Carleton went to the door, opened it and peered outside. Satisfied, he made sure the Do Not Disturb sign was still in place, then closed, locked and bolted the door. Then he went to the closet and took out his garment bag, which he dumped on the bed.

The bag and its contents had been delivered by one of Kohler's lackeys, per Carleton's specifications. It wouldn't have been possible for Carleton to fly in with it, so he made its delivery a condition of his acceptance of the assignment. Apart from Kohler's posturing over the payment of the fee—which Carleton had expected, truth be told—things had gone fairly smoothly. Now, the man was doing just what he'd said he would do. Carleton found that reassuring.

Unzipping the bag, Kohler removed the padded rifle case. He released the latches and flipped it open. Inside, on egg crate foam, were a Glock 19 with two magazines—a formality—and the tool Carleton had selected for this task. It was a simple Remington 700 with variable-power scope, ammunition included. Carleton picked up one of the brass-cased rounds and flipped it across his knuckles with practiced ease.

Time to go to work.

Stony Man Farm, Virginia

KURTZMAN GLANCED at the feed on one of his monitors, turned away and widened his eyes in surprise. He rolled his wheelchair to the interoffice phone and picked it up, stabbing an extension with one calloused finger.

"Price," came the reply.

"Barb," Kurtzman said, "I've just picked up a chatter alert from Homeland Security, a phone line source processed from the Comprehensive Domestic Surveillance program. That character you said Brognola mentioned? His source from Washington?"

"Kearney?"

"That's him," Kurtzman said. "You should see this. The Feds think there's some kind of terrorist threat being made that involves him."

"Terrorists?" Price asked, confused. "Striker isn't hunting terrorists. Hal said this Kearny fellow was tracking vigilantes and the crystal meth trade."

"That's what the feed says," Kurtzman insisted. "Terrorists. This is rated highly credible. We've got to get in touch with Striker."

"I'm on it," Price told him. She punched a number into the phone. "Jack?" she asked. "Are you on standby? Good. You'd better scramble. Coordinate with Bear. We've got an alert and Striker's involved." She pressed another extension, dialed a number from memory. She waited.

THE EXECUTIONER'S HOST directed him to the glass-fronted building facing Clinton Square. It was a modern, well-appointed facility, sitting in the shadow of the *Post Standard*'s much larger headquarters.

Bolan followed Larry Kearney into the lobby of the *Hard Times,* stopping when the larger man turned and looked back at him. "Something's not right," he said. "My guard should be here. He never just leaves."

Bolan's eyes scanned the room. Then he smelled it. "Somebody's fired a weapon in here." The distinct odor of gunsmoke hung in the air.

Kearney drew his Glock, checked it while juggling his cane, then brought the weapon in front of him in a single-hand grip. Bolan brought the 93-R out from under his coat.

Bolan's secure phone began to ring.

The click of a heavy metal safety saved both men.

From the entrance, the Purist who'd been hiding outside leveled a sporter-stock AK rifle at them. Kearney extended his fist and punched two rounds into the man's chest, while Bolan's triple burst caught the biker in the head. He went down like a demolished building, folding in on himself.

Kearney grabbed Bolan's shoulder. "This way!" Beyond the dead man, through the glass doors of the lobby, the pair could see the rear of a tractor trailer headed their way, fast. Bolan shoved Kearney as the larger man hobbled along for all he was worth. They cleared the doors leading to an adjoining corridor just as the trailer crashed through the doors, ramming its way through the front of the building and effectively blocking the way they had come. The entire building shook from the impact. Shards of glass sprayed the lobby and cracked the portholes in the doors behind Bolan and Kearney.

"What the hell are they tryin' to do to me?" Kearney wondered aloud.

"This is just the beginning," Bolan predicted. "Come on. We've got to get out of sight."

"I know just the place," Kearney told him.

TROGG, JACKER AND A FULL mixed force of two dozen Purists and Whiteshirts fanned out through the main office level of the *Hard Times*. They were loaded for bear, shotguns, assault rifles, submachine guns and an assortment of handguns in their fists, on their belts and over their shoulders. Each man wore his biker regalia, or his usual urban togs, with his colors, and each man wore a ski mask—though most of the Whiteshirts had opted for bandannas tied over their faces. Trogg wasn't stupid, not by any means. He was not about to set himself up for life in prison on a terrorism charge. Once their work was done, they would fade in the chaos—and Trogg and those few who made it with him would have enough cash to retire and live like kings. No one would be able to identify him. Sure, they would guess, he thought. They sure as hell would know the Purists had come down on them. They wouldn't be able to prove anything, though, and that was what mattered. He liked the idea of retiring in Mexico, someplace sunny, on the beach. Yeah, someplace he could spend his strong dollars on cheap tequila and pretty *señoritas*. The thought made him smile beneath his mask.

His men stationed outside had blocked off the entrances to the building. A team of four more Purists had secured the basement level, where the printing presses were housed. Two semi trucks and several smaller stolen vehicles had been used to completely barricade the building. Trogg's orders had been clear—make a lot of noise, cause a scene, create a terrorist event the likes of which the Salt City had never even dreamed. The good citizens of Syracuse would talk about this day the way people talked about September 11—dividing their lives between before and after.

Trogg had a couple decades' worth of rage to take out on the city and he was more than happy to oblige the boss. Kohler was a bastard. Trogg was pretty sure he'd had Pick iced somehow, though the others thought it was just Pick's stupid allergy finally claiming him. But he was a *rich* bastard, and Trogg would carry out his orders long enough for payday. He didn't know what the man hoped to gain from this event, but he was footing the bill, and that was all the excuse Trogg needed to stomp the joint flat.

"Get looking," he ordered. "H-Dog, you got that bag?" The Whiteshirt's leader, his face covered by a white bandanna, nodded, gesturing with the heavy duffel bag. "You know where to put 'em."

H-Dog hefted the bag and reached inside, removing one of the Claymore mines. "Front toward enemy, baby," he said, hurrying off to rig the explosives.

A few employees were cowering in their cubicles, under their desks. One of them had tried to play hero, producing a gun of his own. Trogg had personally shot him, claiming the dead man's sweet chromed 1911 as his own. Meeting armed resistance had surprised him.

Trogg was used to his victims being sheep and had been shocked to find a wolf among them. Well, there was one in every crowd, he figured. Stupid, brave—it was all the same, when you pulled on the Purists.

"What you want us to do with these fools, man?" one of the Whiteshirts gestured at the cubicles, cocking his arm up and over, his pistol held sideways in the general direction of the hostages.

"Leave 'em where they are, for now," Trogg said. "They can't get into too much trouble. Try not to kill too many before it's time. We need them till we get the word it's clear to go."

"So we just wait?"

"Yeah. Do whatever."

"I like the sound of that," the Whiteshirt said. He reached over the nearest waist-high cubicle wall and grabbed the woman cowering behind it. She was pretty, wearing a business suit and skirt. "Come on, bitch," the gang member smiled at her past gold-capped teeth. "You and me 'bout to get to know each other."

"Save some for me!" one of the Purists hooted.

Trogg rolled his eyes. He hoped the call came soon. He was hungry.

The Commons, Ithaca, New York

KOHLER EXITED THE CAR and surveyed the scene as Abbot rolled away. He would circle the area until Kohler called him. Neatly dressed in a tailored suit with a sea-blue tie and starched white shirt, Kohler strode forward, attempting to project a confidence he did not feel.

Pedestrian traffic on the Commons was relatively light. There were the usual street musicians, chess players at public tables, clusters of college students and adults who wished they were college students having philosophical conversations. Handmade signs protesting for whatever causes were popular at the moment had been pasted into several shop windows.

He found the man waiting on a wooden bench near the center of the Commons, just where he'd been told he would be.

"You're late," Chang said. His bodyguards sat like stone Buddhas to either side of the diminutive Chang, who might have been thirty or sixty or anywhere in between. Gaunt, sallow and singularly unpleasant, Chang was Kohler's conduit to forces much larger, much more powerful and much more moneyed than was wise to ponder for too long.

"You're early," Kohler came back. He took a bench opposite Chang and swept his gaze over the little man. Chang wore an ill-fitting suit under a trench coat draped like a cape over his shoulders. *He's seen too many Chinese crime lord movies,* Kohler thought. He would have laughed if not for the fact that Chang would have him killed on the spot.

"I agreed to this meeting because you said we would see greater compensation in the future," Chang rasped, his cadence almost singsong despite its menace. "You were told to provide us with a significant amount of the product. You now state that you cannot."

What did the Chinese want with so much methamphetamine anyway? Kohler dismissed the thought. "I've had a production problem," Kohler informed him. "The product we were staging for delivery was tragically lost in a fire. It can be replaced, and it will be. But first I need time to manufacture new product—and to deal with the—unsafe conditions that caused the fire in the first place."

"These fire hazards are not unknown to me," Chang said. "I find your attempts to this point somewhat disturbing in their lack of efficacy."

"I'm sure you know, as well as I, just how difficult it can be to match staff to the challenges offered," Kohler said vaguely. "I assure you, we will solve the problem. Actions have been set in motion that are guaranteed to root out the cause of the problem once and for all."

"This, too, is known to me," Chang said. Kohler doubted that, but then, one never knew. He dismissed the thought, lest it worry him overmuch.

"What I'm asking, most respectfully," Kohler said, "is that you give us more time. Allow us some flexibility in the delivery date. In exchange I will increase the product delivery by ten percent, at no extra cost."

"You ask much. My timetable is not, as you say, flexible."

"Surely," Kohler countered, "you have built into that timetable some room for the unforeseen."

Chang said nothing at first. Finally, he relented. "Perhaps. But I could not possibly allow such leeway for less than...shall we say, forty percent?"

"Now, my dear Comrade Chang—" Kohler shook his head "—let us be reasonable. Even I must operate within certain financial constraints."

Chang's eyes narrowed.

"Let us say twenty percent," Kohler offered.

"Thirty."

Kohler sighed. "You drive a very hard bargain, as they say, Comrade Chang," he said. "Twenty-five percent. That is the limit of what I can manage in time to meet a new deadline."

"We have not set a deadline. Thirty."

"Twenty-five," Kohler said, "and I will have the new shipment to you in four weeks. That gives me enough time to solve my problem, establish the new production facility, employ suitable hired help to guard it and get your product to you."

"Agreed," Chang said, "but it must be two weeks."

"Three," Kohler haggled.

"Enough," Chang said, standing. "It must be two weeks or my use for you will be at an end." He pulled the flaps of his coat around his body, like a vampire preparing for flight.

Kohler stood and faced him. "Two weeks simply is not enough time," he said. This was as close to begging as Kohler would ever come.

"It shall have to be," Chang insisted, "for that is the limit of the *flexibility* in my schedule. Two more weeks is all I can offer. More would bring the displeasure of my government on me, and that would mean my own displeasure would fall on *you*."

Kohler blanched. "Two weeks, then," he said.

Without another word, Chang flapped off, his bodyguards hulking in his wake.

This is not good, Kohler thought.

IT HAD TAKEN ROOK A WHILE to find the perfect spot. He'd settled on an industrial-commercial area on the fringes of the village of Liverpool. There was no pedestrian traffic, and the area was screened from the road by a stand of trees. What was better, the railroad tracks curved around a small hillock that effectively screened the immediate area from view when approached from farther down the tracks.

In the distance, he could hear the horn of the train.

Already, vibrations were being transmitted through the metal of the tracks. Rook put his palm on the metal, felt the approaching steel juggernaut. Perfect.

"What the fuck, man?" one of the Whiteshirts, the more talkative of the two, called plaintively from where he was tightly and thickly duct-taped to his fellow gang member.

"My daughter once confessed to me," Rook told the two Whiteshirts, who even now struggled. They were taped up and stretched across the tracks with their necks on the rails, one man's head taped next to the other man's feet so that only one man's head rested on either side of the tracks. "She admitted to me that she'd been doing drugs. She described it as looking up from the tracks at an oncoming train, hearing the whistle but lacking the strength or the will simply to crawl off the tracks."

"Let us *up,* man!" the talkative one squealed.

"Did you ever leave pennies on the tracks when you were kid?"

"Pennies?" the Whiteshirt said. "What the hell would I do that for, man?"

"Why, to see them flatten, of course. It's an incredible thing, to see a piece of copper shaped like a coin one moment, and find it flat as paper the next. Did you know that since 1982, pennies have been made of mostly zinc? It just isn't the same."

"G-dog, this dude is crazy!" screamed one of the two Whiteshirts. Rook realized he was having trouble telling them apart.

"When I was growing up," he went on, his voice wistful, "there were railroad tracks not far from my house. I spent a lot of happy hours playing near those tracks, watching the trains. I remember that the whole house would shake slightly whenever a train went by. Late at night, I would lie in my bed and feel the house shake, and I grew to love those trains. I would leave coins on the tracks before I went in for dinner, and in the morning I'd find them flattened and stretched. I had an entire cigar box full of those mangled coins."

"Man, this ain't funny!" screamed the other Whiteshirt.

"Did you have model trains as a child?" Rook asked them. "I don't suppose those are very popular in the hood. I had an elaborate set that my father helped me set up on an old picnic table in our basement. I loved that train. It had little shops, tiny telephone poles, hundreds of little details. I can still remember the smell of ozone as that little electric train trundled around on its tracks."

"Please, man, please," the bolder of the two Whiteshirts started begging. "Whatever your beef, man, we can make it right. Let me up. Let me up, man! I'm sorry. I'm sorry, man, for whatever we did to you. Please, just let me go. Please!"

The train was coming closer. The noise was becoming uncomfortably loud. Rook stepped off the tracks, walking slowly, relishing the sound, remembering his childhood, remembering a world when he did not hate himself and wish to die.

As the train came around the bend in the tracks, both gang members let out terrified screams. Rook waved at the train, imagining he could see the engineer even after most of the cars had rumbled past.

Surveying his work, he located the heads of the two Whiteshirts. He glanced about but saw no flattened coins on the bloodied tracks. He regretted bringing no change with him.

No, he thought again, it just wasn't the same.

CARLETON, DRESSED in a black suit, black shirt and silver bolo tie, made his way to the entrance of the Federal Building, crossing a picket line as he did so. The Federal Building was a frequent target for political protestors. Carleton wondered what these people were doing waving signs in front of the building during a workday. Didn't they have jobs?

He carried the padded case for his rifle, and brazenly so. Nothing about it was obviously a rifle case, but of course the Federal Building would have security guards and metal detectors. Fortunately for Carleton, his employer had paved the way.

In the lobby of the building, Carleton caught the eye of one security guard in particular. The guard was bald, of average height and wore wire-frame glasses. He was more or less as Kohler had described. Carleton nodded, then placed a finger by his eye. The guard nodded once in acknowledgment and waved him over.

"I'm here on business," he told the guard.

"Your credentials are in order," the guard told him. Carleton watched as he pressed a button on the side of the metal detector. "Go on," he said.

Carleton nodded and walked through the detector. There was no alarm. None of the other guards noticed him.

Once inside the sterile corridors of the Federal Building, he found the nearest elevator and pressed the button for the uppermost floor. When he exited, he walked as if he belonged there, his gaze fixed on a point well in front of him. Looking beyond those he passed, moving purposefully, he was not challenged. Finally he found the access door to the ladder leading to the roof.

A pleasant if cool breeze was blowing as he made his way across the gravel-lined roof, his expensive leather loafers crunching on the stones. Once he reached the perimeter wall, he looked out over Clinton Square.

Perfect. The view could not be better. Already, Syracuse police cruisers were cordoning off the building containing the *Hard Times* office, lights flashing and sirens blaring. They were chasing off crowds of rubberneckers and trying to keep the press at bay, without much success. It was as Kohler had predicted—chaos.

Smiling, Carleton went about the task of removing the Remington from its padded case. He checked his phone to make sure it was on and had signal, just in case. Then he settled down to wait.

Cortland, New York

THE APARTMENT ON THE SIDE street of the tiny college town of Cortland, New York—home to Tompkins County Community College, or TC3, as it was called by the locals—was little more than a glorified room in what was scarcely more than a glorified boarding house. That was as its occupant, known to his landlady as Aaron Matthews, liked it. The arrangement allowed him to pay his rent in cash, plus a surcharge for the cash payment, two months at a time, up-front. The utilities were in Mrs. Valenza's name, too. Matthews had explained to her that he was having a difficult time with his wife and wished to maintain an apartment for some of his things and as a contingency in case they were unable to work things out. He feared, he told her, that when they did reconcile she might get wind of his renting an apartment and accuse him of lacking commitment, of not truly wanting to work things out. Thus it was imperative that no one, under any circumstances, know that he was working and sleeping there from time to time.

Mrs. Valenza had been almost too happy to keep his secret, lavishing her pity on him, occasionally checking in to see if he was doing all right. He made quite a production of his vague reports to her, affecting a sadness he did not truly feel.

The room was sparsely furnished but equipped for all his needs. He had a kitchenette with a small portable refrigerator, a double sleeping bag on a full-size mattress sitting on the rickety hardwood floor by the bay windows, and his desk. The desk was the only expensive piece of furniture in the room—a multilevel ergonomic model that bore his monitors, color printer, laminator and light table. He had told Mrs. Valenza that he was self-employed and that his work involved creating marketing campaigns and print advertisements.

Matthews worked with only the fading sunlight from the bay windows—the feature of the room he most enjoyed—and the glow from the light table illuminating his efforts. He removed a sheet of passport photos from the printer and eyed it critically. Satisfied, he checked the still unfinished United States Passport to which he would affix his false seal.

Not bad, he thought. Not bad at all. He simply had to complete the delicate process of adding the photo, affixing the seal, and carefully laminating the passport to government specifications, with the appropriate watermarks retained or reapplied, depending on how the original stolen passport held up.

The wireless phone on the desk began to play classical music, softly. He picked it up, examined the caller ID and opened it.

"I'm sorry, I believe you have the wrong number," he said.

"I do not," a voice said in accented English.

"Ah, Comrade Chang," Matthews replied, his voice still cold and flat, betraying no hint of whatever he might be feeling.

"I wish to confirm the date and time of our meeting," Chang said simply.

"It has not changed," Matthews said.

"That is good." Chang did indeed sound pleased. "It is imperative that I receive the package on which we agreed."

"It will be done," Matthews told him.

"Good," Chang said.

"If there's nothing else," Matthews said, in a tone that allowed for no further dialogue, "I really have a lot of work to do."

"Very well." The connection ended.

Matthews closed the phone, smiling and shaking his head. Some clients simply could not resist micromanaging their employees—or their consultants.

"THERE ARE FOUR," Kearney verified in a whisper, peering out from behind the press, where he and Bolan stood in the darkness. He kept his Glock low by his body, at the ready, and leaned on his cane. Behind him, Bolan was exchanging silent text messages with Stony Man Farm.

Kearney had known immediately where the darkest corners were to be found. They'd hustled their way to the basement press level, avoiding several Purist goons along the way. The net was closing as they hurried to the lower levels. They barely made it before the four gang members, walking near them in the darkness, began moving heavy printing equipment to block the exits.

Bolan had seen a play like this often enough—the

Purists were seizing the building, sealing off the perimeter and preparing for a siege. He didn't know why, yet, but it could not be anything good.

The text messages from Barbara Price had started to come in when he'd failed to answer her call. He advised her of the situation and she acknowledged, indicating that Jack Grimaldi had been dispatched. It would take some time for Grimaldi to get there, however; he'd first have to catch a jet from Virginia to Syracuse, where appropriate transportation awaited him at the Syracuse Airport.

Price related, quickly and succinctly, the gist of the chatter report from Homeland Security. It told Bolan what he and Kearney already knew from personal experience—the building was the subject of a major terrorist attack. Price informed him police vehicles, news vans and SWAT teams had surrounded the building and were crowding Clinton Square. Negotiators were bombarding the *Hard Times* with attempts to establish dialogue, transmitted through bullhorns.

When Bolan pressed Price for more details, she transmitted the full text of the DHS report. Bolan showed it to Kearney, whose eyes grew wide. The bulk of the report was a transcription of a domestically surveilled phone call between an unverified contact—tentatively identified as Trogg Sharpe—and one Roger Kohler, in which vague plans for the terrorist attack were outlined.

"Kohler," Kearney whispered. "That son of a bitch. We ran an exposé on his organization last year. He's up to his neck in dirty deals. I don't think he's ever forgiven me."

Bolan, watching over Kearney's shoulder, motioned him to be silent. One of the Purists was edging closer to them, sweeping the shadows with a military-surplus angle-head flashlight.

Kearney looked at Bolan, who nodded. Kearney raised his Glock, tracking the Purist, who passed by without seeing them in the shadows. Kearney glanced back and the Executioner nodded again.

Quietly holstering his Glock, Kearney leaned on one leg and brought up his combat cane. He lunged, whipping out the crook and snaring the passing Purist by the neck. The man made a brief choking noise as he was jerked back, landing heavily on his back with the wind knocked out of him. Kearney brought the cane up and then savagely down again, planting the rubber foot in the Purist's face. The man went limp without another sound.

Kearney nodded.

Bolan passed him, then moved to one side. The two men quietly slipped out of hiding and through the printing room, hunting the three remaining Purists.

Bolan drew his combat knife from its sheath, inverted on his harness. The flat black blade was invisible in the darkness. He moved up on the first Purist he saw, staying clear of the man's flashlight beam.

"Simon!" one of the other bikers yelled from across the room.

The man in front of Bolan turned at the sound of his name. The soldier struck, driving the knife into the man's throat and tearing it free from the side, ducking and stepping at a forty-five-degree angle as he passed the standing dead man. He managed to avoid the spray of blood; Simon went down gurgling.

"Simon?" the voice called again, sounding less certain. "Where did you go, man? You find anything?"

Simon, if he was still alive, was busy bleeding out on the floor of the printing room. He did not answer.

"Lance?" the voice asked.

"Yeah, man, over here." Flashlight beams played across the printing equipment until Lance and his partner found each other. "What is it, Pogue?"

"I can't find Simon."

"Chuckles!" Lance yelled. "You seen Simon?" When there was no answer, Lance raised the Uzi in his hands and let fly. "Stay over there!" he shouted to Pogue. Then he began spraying the room at random. Nine-millimeter rounds ricocheted off printing equipment and punctured the half-height windows set in the walls near the ceiling. Avoiding Pogue—though he didn't seem to be trying all that hard—Lance emptied his magazine, trying to shoot in all directions at once. To his credit, he fired in short bursts, rather than one long, uncontrollable spray.

"I think you got—" Pogue started to say, when a suppressed triple burst from somewhere in the darkness blew his face out the back of his head, with a sizable portion of his brain matter for good measure.

Lance clawed frantically for a spare loaded magazine, trying to drag it out of his belt. Before he could manage it, Larry Kearney came up behind him and clubbed him viciously across the side of the head with the back of his cane's crook, whipping the curved wood into the Purist with his full weight behind the blow. There was a sickening crack as the Purist's skull gave way. He fell as if poleaxed.

"You're trespassing on my property," Kearney grumbled.

Bolan moved quickly, securing the Uzi and the late Lance's spare magazines. He completed the reload the Purist had been attempting and handed the Uzi and the magazines to Kearney.

"Do you know how to use this?" Bolan asked.

Kearney grinned in the darkness, appropriating the flashlight Pogue had dropped, which had rolled near Lance's prone form. "The Sheriffs and I were tight in West Virginia," he explained. "I used to get to play with all their toys, something a mere mortal like me doesn't usually get to do."

"Stay close, then," Bolan told him.

"I'm going to slow you down," Kearney said, gesturing with his cane. "You and I know you'd be better off on your own."

"We do?"

"Hal didn't send me no shrinking violet." Kearney laughed. "We both know what you do."

Bolan said nothing.

Kearney laughed again. "Go on. I'll stay out of the way, do what I can. Don't go getting all worked up if I get my fat ass shot, either. This is my business and I'm not gonna hide while these slime bags walk all over the place. Besides, I have employees in the building. They'll need as much help as we can give them."

Bolan nodded. He and Kearney split up in the connecting corridor, the newsman sticking to the shadows to take the stairs on one end, Bolan making his way to the opposite stairwell in order to take the fight to the enemy.

Somehow, he figured the grumpy old man with the cane would do just fine.

7

Officer Paglia and two dozen other officers, backed up by the city's SWAT team and the special tactics group from the county sheriff's office, stood behind the barricades hastily erected around the *Hard Times* building. He kept his department-issue Smith & Wesson pistol trained on the building, as did most of the other law enforcement personnel. The SWAT team had pulled out all the stops, bringing up an armored breaching vehicle, their MP-5s covering the gang members clustered in the front doorway. One of the city's negotiators was trying to talk to the terrorists through a bullhorn.

"We only want to talk!" he shouted. "No one wants to hurt you! Do you hear me? We want to talk!"

"Screw you!" came the reply. "We're the fucking Central New York Purists, oinkers! This fascist paper is under our control now. Unless you want us to burn it to the ground, you'd best clear out of here!"

Paglia shook his head. It didn't make any sense. The gang members, or terrorists, whatever you wanted to call them, had to know that the police wouldn't just leave. Given the brazen attack on a downtown building—even if the newspaper was a right-wing gossip sheet—there was no way the authorities could allow them to leave. There were two ways out of that building, as far as Paglia was concerned—dead, or in shackles while being marched into a detention van.

GARY ROOK SILENCED THE portable police scanner. From his vantage point behind the wheel of a panel van, he could see the police barricades. The van itself—bearing the logo of the local cable company—was stolen, expendable. He'd carjacked it from an employee not far from the railroad tracks, leaving the driver in a nearby Dumpster. He'd felt nothing about putting a .45 slug in the cable guy's brain. He couldn't have the man reporting the theft of the van before Rook was through with it. He'd thought, originally, that he might feel guilty about it, if only a little, but he felt nothing. The man had been an obstacle and that obstacle had been removed.

No one paid him any attention as he sat parked illegally on the corner, far enough back to be out of the way. He'd heard it on the news—there were news vans surrounding him, broadcast array extended—and the police scanner had confirmed it. The Purists had taken the *Hard Times* building, they had hostages and they were making plenty of demands. He'd been driving aimlessly when the first reports trickled in over the AM talk station he kept on for noise. It was like a sign from God, like a message from Jennifer. The Purists were there, maybe not all of them, but certainly most of them. All of them, conveniently in one place—his mouth almost watered at the thought of catching them confined there.

The police and SWAT teams had the Purists effectively pinned down, but they were also keeping Rook *out*. If he was to get in there, if he was truly to take his revenge and attain Jennifer's justice, he had to figure out how to get past them. They'd shoot him if he tried to walk in there, or at least stop him. Either way, he would fail and he'd lose his chance. That couldn't happen.

What to do? What to do? Rook chewed his nails, watching the building, brow furrowed. He had to think of a way.

TROGG TRIED HARD NOT TO laugh. Jacker was really outdoing himself, spouting every cliché he could remember from every hostage movie he'd ever watched. Trogg snickered when Jacker got to the part about wanting a helicopter and fifty million dollars. The man might as well have asked for a busload of hookers riding unicorns, for all he was likely to get. It wouldn't matter. Trogg figured they had at least a few hours while the cops tried to talk them out, and Jacker was doing his best to make it clear that this was a Purist operation. Kohler had been adamant on that point, and Trogg understood the strategy. It wouldn't hurt to have the name of the Purists shouted from the rooftops, either. When they were done, Trogg and his men would be paid and Kohler would get whatever it was he wanted from this little operation. Trogg knew that at least one of the man's goals was to eliminate the guy who'd been hitting the Purists.

Trogg knew Kohler didn't give a damn about the Purists, but he needed them. The bikers were his link to the crank he wanted, for whatever reason he wanted it. The Purists had a big problem with the trigger-happy shit head who killed Chopper Mike and his family, not to mention blowing up the cook house. Kohler figured he was doing them a big favor, probably, by eliminating that big problem—and he was helping himself in the bargain. Trogg knew that Kohler would sell them all out and even kill them personally if that was the way to get what he wanted. For now, though, their goals were the same. Trogg wanted revenge. Kohler wanted the crank. Everybody who mattered would be happy.

And everybody else would be dead.

THE EXECUTIONER STALKED the masked gang member who wore a baggy white T-shirt and had a white bandanna over his face. He was accompanied by two others, who were helping him set up Claymore mines at likely entry points. Bolan's eyes had narrowed when he saw the military hardware. If the police got overeager and tried to breach the building, the ball bearings contained in the Claymores would be there to greet them at high speed, turning them to hamburger.

Working his way in the wake of gang members, he'd found three other Claymore emplacements in stairwells and had quietly reversed each one. It had been tricky pursuing them without making his presence known, but as the group removed the last of the Claymores and wadded up the bag that had contained them, Bolan's wait was over. He paused until the masked Whiteshirt armed the mine and turned from it. Then he stepped out from behind the corner of the last stairwell. The Whiteshirts were already trotting up the stairs. Bolan stepped quietly to the mine, walking behind them, stopping to switch the Front Toward Enemy so it pointed at the retreating thugs.

He could have shot them from behind, but the angle was poor. He needed to get them all and could not afford to have a straggler running back to report his presence to the others.

"Hey!" he yelled, the Beretta 93-R pointed up the stairwell. "Drop your weapons and put your hands in the air!"

The Whiteshirts stopped. They turned and faced him.

"H-Dog, man," one of the Whiteshirts muttered, "he got us."

"Yeah, he got us," H-Dog replied. His hands were behind his back. "Oh, he got us bad. You best put down yo' straps."

The other Whiteshirts exchanged glances.

H-Dog started to move.

"I wouldn't," Bolan told him.

H-Dog slapped the Claymore detonator three times. Bolan dropped back, ears smarting, as the shaped-charge mine spewed its deadly contents at the Whiteshirts, tearing them to pieces and pocking the concrete stairs and the wall beyond them in countless places. The coppery smell of blood was suddenly heavy in the air.

"I warned you," Bolan said to the bloody mess.

IT WAS THE SWAT TEAM THAT gave Rook his in. He had been thinking, as he sat impatiently in the truck, that the armament he carried himself was not terribly different from the hardware sported by the SWAT troopers, whose arms were a mixture of MP-5s and AR-15s. It then occurred to him that he had a set of black BDUs and a surplus Kevlar helmet in the back of the van. With the camo cover removed, the helmet would look close enough to the SWAT headgear to pass from a distance.

Climbing into the back of the van, Rook changed his clothes. He secured his .45s in their holsters under his BDU blouse, tucking the belt holsters for the Smith & Wessons under the blouse, as well. Fortunately, the uniform was just slightly too large for him, as he'd purposely bought the biggest he could get to accommodate his large frame. With the helmet on and his CAR-15 across his chest on its single-point sling, he'd look just like the rest of the SWAT personnel, as long as no one inspected him too closely.

Carefully exiting the van, he made sure no one saw a SWAT cop leaving a cable van. Then he held his head high and walked with a practiced swagger as he made his way across Clinton Square, to the barricades. He kept his gaze fixed on the building, moving among the other cops and SWAT people as if he belonged there. From the rear of the armored breaching vehicle, hunkered down for protection from gunfire, was the chief of police himself, Michael Gray.

Gray was on his phone and looked troubled. "Are you sure?" he heard Gray say. "There's no going back if we do."

Gray signaled Commander Heaney, who was in

charge of SWAT on site and of coordinating the special tactics groups with the Syracuse police. Gray waved the phone and nodded to it, trying to be subtle. "It's time," he told Heaney. "You're going in."

Heaney checked the AR-15 across his chest. He looked at Gray. "You're positive?"

"Go," Gray said.

"Come on," Heaney said as he trotted toward the front of the barricade, addressing a SWAT trooper he did not recognize. Rook nodded and fell in behind him.

"Listen up!" Heaney said when he reached the barrier. "We're going in hot. Assemble your people and prepare to take out those assholes in the front entrance."

FROM THE ROOFTOP OF THE Federal Building, Carleton frowned behind his scope. He saw the SWAT troops mobilizing and understood exactly what was happening. This, too, had been part of Kohler's plan, at least as it had been described to Carleton. What bothered him was that there was no sign of the vigilante for whom Carleton was here. Kohler had been convinced that this whole spectacle would be more than the killer could resist. Like a pervert passing a playground, he'd *have* to come looking—wouldn't he?

If there was no target, Carleton realized he wouldn't get paid. That bastard Kohler would probably insist on getting at least some of the down payment returned, too. Damned if he'd hand back any of that money, Carleton thought. He was owed extra, as far as he was concerned, for being forced to travel out here to the back end of nowhere in frigging Syracuse, for crying out loud.

HEARING THE SOUND OF AN explosion from somewhere behind them, Jacker got nervous. Whatever was happening inside the building, it seemed as if they were losing control. Jacker spoke to Wheelie, the Purist backing him up on door duty. Two Whiteshirts waited with them, AKs at the ready, in case the cops tried to rush the entrance.

"Bring me the launcher!" he said.

One of the Whiteshirts brought the Russian RPG tube, while the other brought the bag full of rocket-propelled grenades. Jacker put the weapon to his shoulder, wrapping his fist around the pistol grip, and lined up on the nearest police cruiser.

OFFICER PAGLIA SAW the trail of smoke and threw himself to the ground. The police cruiser only yards away was blown onto its side, then rolled onto its hood, smoke and fire erupting as shrapnel from the vehicle flew in all directions. Nearby, the line of SWAT troopers preparing to breach the building crouched low, then filed behind the armored breaching vehicle. The officers who were able started to fire on the main entrance of the building. Paglia shook off the effects of the explosion, dropped to a low crouch and started firing.

The Purist was reaching for another rocket-propelled grenade, when the firestorm of hot lead caught him. The hail of gunfire ripped through his body and smacked into the Whiteshirts behind him, ripping them apart and spraying the wall behind them with their blood.

"Go! Go! Go!" Commander Heaney ordered, motioning his combined SWAT and special operations personnel to take the building. "First team, left side! Second team, right side!" The first team was his own. The second team was composed of the sheriff's department troopers. He led the way himself, his AR-15 held at the ready as he advanced in an aggressive crouch.

In the confusion and the gunplay, no one noticed when Gary Rook slipped inside the building with the team and disappeared.

THE EXECUTIONER BURST through the door to the upper level of the *Hard Times* building, where he found several Purists and Whiteshirts lounging about in the small cafeteria and meeting-room area. One of the vending machines had been broken open and the gang members were gorging themselves on snacks and candy bars, their masks removed or pulled up over their mouths. Heel-toe stepping in a combat crouch, Bolan took an aggressive Isosceles stance and brought the Beretta 93-R to bear, moving as fast he could while accurately engaging targets.

The gang members went for their weapons. Bolan thumbed his weapon to single shot and double-tapped the first Purist, then the second, then turned forty-five degrees and moved to the left, his hand balled into a fist against his chest and his weapon extended one-handed in his right. Still moving, he double-tapped a third Purist, then a Whiteshirt, then another Whiteshirt. His steps had taken him across the room and behind the cover of the vending machine, which absorbed sporadic fire from the two gang members still standing. Bolan transferred the 93-R to his left fist, backed off from the vending machine about a yard, and crouched on his left knee as he leaned out on the left-hand side of the sparking, smoking machine. Expecting him to come from the right, the two Purists were caught unaware. Bolan punched two rounds into the first and three more into the second.

The entire maneuver had taken only seconds. With practiced ease, Bolan ejected the Beretta's magazine, reloaded and recovered the dropped extra rounds as he knelt while still sweeping the room for threats. He secured the partial in his combat harness. You never knew when those few extra rounds would make a difference.

Satisfied, Beretta still at the ready in a two-hand grip, the Executioner moved on.

WITH CHAOS ERUPTING, Trogg instinctively went lower, his great bulk thundering down the stairs and crashing through the metal doors that led to the basement-level presses.

Once there, he moved behind the nearest piece of large machinery, his Colt Python in one meaty fist, ready for anything. Trogg knew when to save his own skin—and he knew when to teach a man a final, violent lesson.

The door slapped open and Trogg opened fire—only to see no one.

Larry Kearney, behind the door but now aware of Trogg's position, shoved the door again, this time stumbling through it with his Glock leading the way. He emptied the magazine in Trogg's direction, keeping the biker pinned down. As the slide on the Glock locked back, Kearney threw the weapon, striking Trogg flat in the face. The big man howled and grabbed his face, dropping his Colt. Then Kearney was on him, striking with his lacquered combat cane, the curved crook whistling through the air smacking into the Purist with lethal intent. Trogg shrieked, curling into himself.

"You…are going to pay…for what you did…to my people…and our place of business!" Kearney vowed between two-handed sledgehammer blows. Trogg rolled over and Kearney brought the cane down with all his might—cracking the shaft.

The split down the cane, from force it was never designed to endure, was accompanied by the resounding crack of something inside Trogg's ribs or spine. The gang leader made a gurgling noise as blood welled up from his mouth and out his nose.

"Take that, you murdering son of a bitch," Kearney said with satisfaction. He waited—Trogg's mammoth form did not move. The big man lay on his stomach, an inert mountain of flesh.

Kearney hobbled closer toward where the Glock had fallen, the slide locked open. He bent to retrieve it.

Trogg, as quick as a rattlesnake, reached out and clamped one meaty fist around Kearney's wrist, pulling him heavily to the ground. Kearney hit the floor and his head bounced from concrete. He saw stars floating in his vision.

"I'm gonna to rip your arms out," Trogg bubbled through bloody breaths, his eyes wild. "I'm gonna make you wish you was never born." He grabbed hold of

Kearney's throat and started to squeeze. Kearney felt his vision dim around the edges as white noise rushed through his ears.

Then he felt nothing.

GARY ROOK FOUND Trogg Sharpe in the basement, choking the life out of some old man. "Glad to see you're still a man who likes a challenge," he said, his voice hollow.

Trogg looked up from the man he'd choked unconscious. "This bad old dude almost *killed* me, man!" he gurgled. Blood poured from his mouth.

Rook took a step closer, his combat-booted footfalls heavy in the darkened room. The light mounted to Rook's CAR-15 illuminated the wounded biker. He brought the weapon up, where the bottom tip of its stock had never left his shoulder, and aimed at the bloodied face.

"Hey, man," Trogg begged. "What are you frigging doing? You gotta take me in." He wheezed, unable to stand, half kneeling, half bent over the prone form of the man he'd been choking.

"I don't have to take you in," Rook informed him, shuffling a step closer.

"But you're the *cops*," Trogg said plaintively.

"I'm not the cops," Rook said, his voice dead. He shuffled another step closer, his carbine still pointed at Trogg's face. The gang leader squinted, but one of his pupils was dilated. He was already dying from the beating he'd taken.

Trogg looked at Rook, not understanding. Rook couldn't have that. Trogg Sharpe *had* to understand, before he died.

Rook fished in one of his pockets and produced a photograph. He flipped it to Trogg, who could not catch it. The big man stared down at the photo. A corner was dipped in his own blood as it pooled around him on the floor. The girl in the photo meant nothing to him.

"That was my Jennifer," Rook told him. "She was the only thing I had left. She was the only good person left in my life. She was all I had to remind me what I used to be, who I used to be. She was my only link to everything that was ever good and the only hope that anything might be good again. You *took* her from me. Your filthy drugs ate her up, made her eat *herself* up, left her a walking, toothless skeleton. It's because of you, because of parasites like you, that she's dead.

"I can't bring her back," Rook said finally, "but I can bring her justice. I'm going to be the one to send you to hell, Trogg."

"It ain't me!" Trogg cried, his voice clogged with fluid. "I'm not the guy! Kohler, that's who you want! The…the rich land man…Kohler!"

Staring down the barrel of a gun, Trogg reached for the name as if it were a talisman, magic that could save his life. "Kohler, man, Kohler!"

Shaken, Rook wavered—as did the barrel of his weapon. Could it be? He'd long suspected there was big money behind the Purists—but Roger Kohler? The man was a leading figure in Syracuse.

As Rook hesitated, Trogg took his chance. His thick

hand went clumsily for the chromed .45 still in his belt. The weapon came up—

Rook, startled, brought the CAR-15 back on target.

As both weapons fired—Larry Kearney, roaring, surged to his knees and brought the crook half of his broken cane forward in an arc, from low at his side. The pointed crook hooked Trogg's left eyeball and buried itself deep in the gang leader's skull as Kearney, still yelling, shoved the much bigger man backward. The biker fell on his back, a slain giant. Kearney dragged himself clear of the pool of Sharpe's blood and collapsed, still clutching the other half of his broken combat cane.

"First thing...I'm going to do," he said, breathless, "is buy me...another one...of these canes." He passed out.

Rook, shocked, checked himself for injuries. Sharpe's bullet had missed him. Reeling, not sure if he felt relieved, vindicated, or cheated of his revenge, he fled.

As the SWAT team cleared the main floor and the upper levels, Heaney was trying very hard to grasp what he was seeing. They'd found no less than three bloody stairwells where the terrorists had tried to set off Claymore mines as the SWAT team closed in. In the fourth, which had been abandoned completely, they found a Claymore sitting backward, pointing toward the stairs instead of out toward the team. Could the gang members, or whoever they were, really have been that stupid?

There were a few casualties among the *Hard Times*

staff. A couple of the male staffers had been shot. The owner, Larry Kearney, had been found in the basement, where he'd apparently fought off Trogg Sharpe himself, killing the man. What was supposed to be the worst terrorist attack in Onondaga County—and a hostage situation on which Heaney could capitalize—was over, with most of the fighting done by people other than the law-enforcement personnel at the scene. There was no way Heaney could execute the surviving staff members, or Kearney, or the mysterious gunman to whom Kohler had referred. There was no ongoing battle to cover it. He had no choice but to play it straight, doing his job and hoping to hell Kohler wouldn't exact revenge when the SWAT commander explained the situation to his sometime employer.

Heaney almost recoiled when the gunman found him. The big, dark-haired man stared through Heaney with an intensity that made the SWAT leader nervous.

"Cooper," Bolan told him. "Justice Department."

"Heaney," the Commander responded. "County SWAT."

"What we have here, commander," Bolan told him, "is a failed terrorist attempt, foiled in no small part through the bravery of the owner of the place."

"That is what I understood, yes," Heaney said. Kearney was outside the building already, being treated by the paramedics. He was winded, exhausted and sore, but had sustained no permanent injuries. Media people had lined up around him three deep and were already feting him as a hero.

BOLAN MADE HIS WAY OUT of the building, as various

law-enforcement personnel mopped up. At the front entrance, he caught Paglia's eye and nodded. The officer stood by a burning police cruiser. Several fire units were on the scene and one was dousing the flaming wreckage.

The Executioner was disappointed. He was relieved to learn that Kearney was all right and pleased that they could put an end to the occupation of the building, but something about it simply didn't add up. It might be more accurate to say that something about it added up all too well, actually. The more Bolan thought about it, the more it sounded like an elaborate setup. The Purists had seized the building and made their presence very loudly, very violently known. While Kearney had given them plenty of cause to dislike him, this sort of all-or-nothing play seemed out of proportion to their beef with the newspaper man.

It would, however, make the perfect draw if someone wanted to lure the vigilante killer out of hiding.

That had to be it. As Bolan considered it, it made more and more sense. The Purists had gone on the offensive and apparently brought in backup—Kearney had explained the arm's-length relationship between the Purists and the Whiteshirts. They'd staged an elaborate show, probably enjoying the violence for its own sake and for the publicity, but what they'd really wanted was for Gary Rook to show up so they could take him out. They'd tried an ambush before—

Bolan frowned. They hadn't staged the show for

Rook. They had staged it for Bolan, mistaking him for the vigilante.

Bolan glanced around. Could Rook be here, somewhere? Had he been here? Bolan and Kearney had managed to kill the Purists and Whiteshirts themselves, with a little help from the cops outside. Rook had been denied what he was seeking—a final accounting with the gang members. Now Trogg was dead. Did that mean it was over?

Bolan took out his phone and dialed the secure number for Stony Man Farm.

THROUGH THE SCOPE OF HIS rifle, Carleton saw the man Kohler had described, the man whose activities had been detailed in the dossier first delivered by the poor, unfortunate Pick. Relieved that he'd be collecting his fee after all, the high-priced assassin waited patiently for the vigilante to stop moving through the crowd. Carleton watched as the tall man stopped and took out his phone.

Carleton breathed, getting into the zone. He cleared his mind, focused on the target. Exhaling half a breath and holding it, every muscle in his body relaxed and ready, he allowed his index finger to tighten, the pad of his finger pressing the face of the trigger. He squeezed, knowing that when the glass-rod-breaking feel of the trigger came to him, it would surprise him, as it should. He felt nothing but the rifle. He heard nothing, did not notice the increasing noise, the air currents whipping around him, the rhythmic pulse surrounding him.

Wait for it—

The roar and the wind was like the sudden howl of an angered god. Carleton immediately rolled onto his back, covering his face with one arm, the rifle clutched across his body. Above him, the Bell AH-1 Cobra hovered as the pilot brought the three-barreled, electrically driven, 20 mm General Dynamics rotary cannon to bear.

Carleton, seeing no choice, whipped the Remington to his shoulder.

Before he could shoot, the cannon's projectiles shredded his body and hurled what was left over the side of the Federal Building.

8

Ithaca, New York

Chang sat behind the expensive desk in his well-appointed office. The only light came from the antique green glass lamp on the desk. It cast a feeble globe of dim light that cast his face in dark, unflattering relief, deepening the lines of his long, sallow face and hooding his eyes in pools of shadow. A silver cigarette case and a polished silver lighter rested on the desk. A silver ashtray overflowing with unfiltered butts smoldered near his right hand.

"Sit down, please," Chang told his guest. "Would you care for one?" He gestured, removing a cigarette for himself. His guest took one and produced his own lighter—a tarnished brass Zippo—firing the smoke to life and taking a long drag before expelling it through his nose.

"Comrade Chang," his guest said finally.

"Comrade Song," Chang acknowledged. "How are things in the People's Liberation Army?"

"The same." Song nodded. He looked positively uncomfortable in civilian clothes, dressed as he was to blend in while visiting Chang's base of operations. The location obviously puzzled him; a small college town in rural upstate New York hardly seemed the place to launch an operation of this scope.

"You would not be here if Beijing were not concerned," Chang said, lighting his cigarette and pausing to breathe in the smoke with relish.

"True," Song admitted. "There is concern that the plan can be brought off as you conceived it. The timetable is in jeopardy."

"Perhaps," Chang admitted. "Perhaps not. If Roger Kohler cannot provide the methamphetamine we require, we will locate it elsewhere and find a plausible reason for shipping it in."

"We could have manufactured it ourselves."

"We could have, yes," Chang agreed, "at the risk of discovery. Need I remind you that we must be able to point to domestic sources of the components? This particular formula will work, and work well. We have constructed a reasonable explanation for its existence and we have accounted for its other constituent chemicals—with the exception of the methamphetamine. It must come from this country. It must be the sort of thing domestic terrorists could obtain, something they could use. We must give the Americans a template they can readily accept—another Oklahoma City. Even if he fails to provide the methamphetamine, Kohler has done us a service in his failure. He has raised the specter of terrorism here, by Americans and perpetrated on Americans. Here, among the cows and the college children."

"It does make sense," Song concurred, "but without the methamphetamine we cannot complete the formula."

"As I said, I can make other arrangements," Chang reassured him. "Do not underestimate the power of fear. Kohler may yet provide what we need. I have instilled sufficient fear in him. We may be surprised by the results. It would amuse me to find that he has hurt himself in order to fulfill his obligations."

"Better to be feared than loved when one of the two must be lacking," Song said, paraphrasing Machiavelli.

"Really, Song," Chang laughed, "I did not realize you were so broadly educated. Should not a scion of the People's Liberation Army quote Sun Tzu instead?"

"Talking is talking," Song said. "Fighting is fighting."

"Fair enough." Chang shrugged.

Song rose. "You will keep me informed. I must make regular reports to Beijing."

"I will keep you informed," Chang promised. Song left, closing the door quietly behind him.

Chang sat in silence, contemplating the darkness. Finally, he reached for his phone.

IN HIS SMALL OFFICE in the administration building at Ithaca College, Zhongchao Hu sat at his battered desk, methodically checking and double-checking files on his laptop. His position as events coordinator for the college kept him busy, that was true. There was a time, not so long ago, when he had actually entertained thoughts of living out his days as an academic before retiring and living on his pension.

Those hopes had been dashed eight months ago, when the phone call he had been dreading for fifteen years had finally come.

"You are activated," the voice had said. Hu, sitting in the living room of his small home in Ithaca, had turned ashen as he listened.

It had happened. They had finally found a use for him.

Hu, as a sleeper agent of the People's Republic of China, had emigrated to the United States and pursued a career in academia on the orders of his government. He had insinuated himself in the bureaucratic structure as part of a long-term plan to gain control of American popular culture.

It was the type of far-reaching, perhaps unattainable plan for which the power structure in Beijing was known. Hu had done his part, with fervent and zealous dedication at first, and then more out of habit, as he grew to like the comforts of his position and started to find his life in America more to his liking than he did his Spartan existence in China. Ideally, he was to live out his life doing his best to affect America's future, converting the nation from within by preaching to and converting its youth.

He was not so naive as to think he was not monitored. When the opportunity arose, they knew just how to use him, just how to leverage his position. Hu had granted Chinese agents access to lab facilities they needed at the college—facilities that would allow them to maintain the domestic facade that cloaked the operation. It was Zhongchao who had arranged for the target of the operation. He would provide the details of the event security, who would provide the appropriate passes so the necessary individuals could gain access to the event.

Hu was the key to the operation, really.

It was an honor. It was supposed to be an honor, at any rate. Hu did not feel honored—for when it ended, he would have the choice of returning to China or going to jail.

His phone rang. He quickly answered the call.

"Yes?" he said tentatively.

"All is in readiness?" Chang asked without preamble.

"Yes," Hu reported. "The facilities are ready. I have arranged for the proper credentials. We require only the arrival of your people—and of the final components. All else is on site."

"You will be informed," Chang said. "Our timetable may be delayed."

"We have just over two weeks," Hu reminded him. "The date of the visit is set. It cannot be changed."

"I am aware of that," Chang told him. "I am simply keeping you informed. Be prepared to move quickly when the time comes, so the opportunity is not lost."

"I will."

"For the people," Chang said.

"For the people," Hu replied. He glanced at the phone's digital display. Chang had already hung up.

Syracuse, New York

SEATED IN THE SPACIOUS backseat of Larry Kearney's lovingly maintained 1992 Cadillac Brougham, Mack

Bolan and Jack Grimaldi looked out the window at the office building on the corner of Jefferson and Salina.

"This is the place," Kearney told his passengers from the driver's seat. "Diamond Corporation headquarters is on the top floor of this building. One Roger Kohler is the CEO and, as I live and breathe, that is the name that waste of skin gave whoever it was that saved my ass in that basement."

"Are we proceeding on the theory that the man was Gary Rook?" Grimaldi asked.

"I don't see why not," Kearney put in. "I couldn't rightly see him—I couldn't see much of anything—but it had to be him. He's had a day to figure it out. Frankly, I'm surprised he didn't show up here already."

"He could be in there right now," the Stony Man pilot suggested. "What do you say, big guy? Should we have brought the Cobra with us? I hated to give up that chopper."

"You made record time getting here and I can't fault your entrance," Bolan told him, "but I think mounting a chopper assault on an office building downtown would be a little much. As it was, the Syracuse police and their federal counterparts were ready to force me out or lock me up. Hal had to intervene again."

"He just loves doing that," Grimaldi said, chuckling. He checked the sawed-off shotgun he carried under his windbreaker. "We going in?"

"I'll wait in the car," Kearney said. "I think I've had enough excitement for about three lifetimes."

"Thanks for your help," Bolan said, reaching over the seat to shake his hand. "With any luck, it will be just Kohler up there and there won't be any fireworks."

"You and luck?" Kearney said skeptically. "Forget it. I'll move the car so the building doesn't fall on it."

Bolan checked the Beretta and the Desert Eagle in his combat harness, once again hidden beneath his coat. He and Grimaldi exited the car and walked casually into the office building, Grimaldi doing his best to hide the shotgun. In the lobby, which was empty, Bolan noted the Diamond Corporation logo on the office listing. It was indeed on the top floor.

"Let's go," he said. They took the elevator and Grimaldi pressed the button. The doors closed.

Gary Rook, a trench coat over his BDUs, entered the lobby.

ROGER KOHLER SAT BEHIND his desk, his head in his hands.

It had all gone so very wrong.

Trogg and all his people were dead. That was not such a problem—he could set up a new lab, even find the right sort of criminal element to run it. He might even be able to do it on a tight timetable, if he contracted out. There were suppliers in Nevada and Florida, people he knew, contacts he'd made. He would have to pay an exorbitant sum, possibly even take a loss. He knew he could not afford that loss—but he could afford making an enemy of Chang and his government even less. Like it or not, he was on the hook for the meth. He would have to find a way to make the shipment. He would pay any price, cut any deal. He couldn't recoup his losses or enjoy his profit margin if Chang cut off his head, hands and feet before dumping what was left in a ditch somewhere.

It had started out bad and only got worse. The vigilante who'd started all this, the bastard who'd thrown the wrench into the machinery of Kohler's intricate plan, was still out there somewhere. Carleton, his highly paid assassin, hadn't just failed, he'd been discovered and killed in spectacular fashion.

Kohler knew how to connect the dots. Enough forces were arrayed against him that it was likely the Feds, the law and a cast of hundreds—including the Internal Revenue Service—were fast on his heels. For the second time in as many hours he seriously considered the Korth revolver sitting in the velvet-lined box in his desk drawer. One bullet and he could put all this behind him—but what a *waste* of his potential!

Standing to look out the window, Kohler folded his hands behind his back and permitted himself a single sigh. His father would have beaten him soundly for falling prey to self-pity. He resolved to cast off his doubts and his recriminations, his anxieties and his fears. He was Roger Kohler and, by God, he would face his fate as a man, with his head held high. He would go down fighting if he had to. His first order of business, however, was to deal with the immediate threat. Chang had to be pacified. The shipment had to be made.

Kohler turned with sudden determination. It would be Nevada. He would start with his contacts there.

He was reaching for the desk phone when his office door burst open.

"You!" he said.

"Me," Bolan said simply. The Desert Eagle was in his fist, pointed at Kohler's heart.

Kohler's shoulders slumped and he looked away, out the window. Then he stood to his full height, smoothed his tailored suit and looked Bolan in the eye. "Tell me who you are."

Bolan was silent.

"Why?" Kohler pressed. "What did the Purists do to you? They're scum, yes, and probably better off dead in the grand scheme of things. But what of the others? The women, the children? Surely you're not so heartless a man as to be capable of those things."

"You and your Purists got it wrong," Bolan said. "I was never hunting them, not directly. I'm not the vigilante."

Kohler gaped. "Then how—"

"Trogg Sharpe gave you up," Bolan told him. "The vigilante squeezed it out of him. He could be on his way here right now. I'm the only thing standing between you and him."

Kohler struggled to wrap his mind around the idea.

"Now," Bolan told him, "it's time you explained what this is all about."

Kohler's shoulders sagged again. "Fine," he said. "I'll tell you everything. May I sit?"

Bolan shrugged.

Kohler slumped into his chair.

Gunshot sounded from the outer office, followed by the thunderclap of a shotgun blast.

Kohler went for the desk drawer. Bolan was faster, punching a .44 slug through the man's shoulder. The businessman spun in his chair, screaming, blood pouring from his wound. Bolan was on him, ripping open the desk drawer and finding the Korth. He removed it and shoved it into his belt.

"Sarge!" Grimaldi called from the outer office. "You better get in here!"

Bolan kicked the door open on its two-way hinges, casting a warning glance back at Kohler. He found Grimaldi with the shotgun trained on Gary Rook, who stood with the receptionist held by the thoat. His Smith & Wesson was at her temple, the hammer thumbed back.

"Well, if it isn't Captain America!" Rook scoffed. "This is familiar."

"Don't," Bolan ordered him. "Nothing is worth this many innocent lives."

"It isn't?" Rook asked. "Tell that to my Jennifer! Worth it? Hero, you don't know where I've been."

Grimaldi glanced at Bolan, who glanced back and then looked over his shoulder to check on Kohler. The businessman was still behind his desk. Bolan assessed the situation. Grimaldi's shotgun was too imprecise; he couldn't take the man without hitting the woman. Bolan could shoot, but he was back where he started; he could not be sure Rook wouldn't pull the trigger as he died.

"I don't know where you've been?" Bolan said, buying time. "You'd be surprised. Nobody understands your pain better than me. I know what it's like to lose people you care about, to see them torn from you, to see them shot down. It's why I do what I do."

"Then face Kohler with me!" Rook demanded. "How can any man not want him dead? He's a parasite! He grows fat off the people of this county while sucking the life out of them. He trades in drugs! He's dirty to his eyeballs—and that means he's just as responsible for Jennifer's death as that biker trash and their filthy allies were. You helped me! You helped me kill them…help me now!"

"You crossed the line," Bolan told him, inching closer. "Innocent people are dead."

"Justice!" Rook shrieked.

"Revenge, not justice," Bolan told him. "Give me the gun."

Behind Bolan, Kohler bolted.

"No!" Rook shouted. He swung his revolver toward Kohler.

Bolan stepped in, grabbed the weapon and the hand that gripped it, then clubbed Rook on the side of the head with the barrel of the Desert Eagle. He used his own shoulder as leverage to snap Rook's arm in an arc, levering the weapon out of his grasp. The receptionist shrieked and ran when she saw her opening.

"Jack!" Bolan yelled, struggling with Rook, "Go for Kohler!"

Grimaldi ran without a word.

The Desert Eagle was pried out of his grasp as he fought with Rook. Both men tried to draw another weapon, but they were well matched. Each fought the other and prevented the draw as they struggled, crashing into the receptionist's desk and clinching up. Bolan kicked savagely; Rook blocked with his own legs and kicked back. Bolan tried to wrestle Rook to the floor and went for a head butt, but the other man was ready for it and neither fighter managed a telling blow.

"Get off me!" Rook yelled. "Can't you see he's getting away?"

"It ends here," Bolan told him.

GRIMALDI, SHOTGUN AT THE ready, ran headlong down the street, chasing Roger Kohler. The businessman ran as if the devil himself were in pursuit. Pedestrians dodged or gawked as they shot past. It was likely at least one citizen with a cell phone had called the police. Grimaldi had a moment to wonder if the Justice credentials in his pocket would pass muster.

The Stony Man pilot dodged a mailbox and pushed past a knot of women in business suits crossing the street. Kohler was still ahead, running full-out, showing no signs of tiring. Grimaldi found himself worrying if the other man was in better shape. He was starting to feel a bit winded himself.

Two Syracuse police cruisers came out of nowhere, burning around a side street and pulling up to cut off Kohler's escape. Grimaldi slowed to a walk and approached, careful to keep the shotgun low and pointed to the ground.

"You!" one of the officers yelled. "Drop that weapon! Get on the ground!"

"Justice Department!" Grimaldi yelled back, kneeling to comply. "Detain that man!"

They'd get everything sorted out back at the station. Brognola was going to love that.

IN DIAMOND'S OFFICES, the battle raged. Rook was strong, fearless, and fast—a match for Bolan in most respects, making up in ferocity what he lacked in technique. The Executioner was used to ending his fights quickly. When Rook did not go down, he had to reevaluate. He could not afford to duel this man, to fight a war of attrition as they hammered away at each other. He needed to bring this to a close. With each passing minute, the chance that Rook could win, or simply gain the leverage he needed to escape, increased.

As they reeled into Kohler's office, Rook's eyes went wide. Bolan could follow the man's thoughts—the vigilante was watching his chance at final revenge slip away. Bolan let go with one hand and smashed Rook against the jaw, but the other man simply absorbed it and tried an upper cut followed by a knee. Bolan blocked, kneed Rook twice himself and shoved the other man back.

They collided with the window through which Kohler had been gazing only moments before.

The glass gave under their combined weight and momentum. Bolan was able to catch himself on the frame. Rook plummeted through without a sound.

FROM THE DRIVER'S SEAT of his Cadillac, Larry Kearney watched as a shower of glass pelted a parked SUV in front of the building housing the Diamond offices. The glass fragments were followed by a large man in a trench coat, who hit the SUV so hard that he collapsed the roof and shattered every pane of glass in the vehicle.

"I knew there was a good reason to move the car," Kearney muttered as he reached for his phone to dial 911.

9

Roger Kohler sat at the scarred metal interrogation table, a cup of coffee sitting untouched by his right elbow. He stared into space, contemplating his fate.

They'd read him the litany when they brought him in. It was as bad as he'd thought, and worse. Department of Homeland Security had complete transcripts and recordings of his dealings with Trogg Sharpe—and of one cryptic conversation he'd had with the man they did not yet know was Chang. He was being charged with conspiracy to commit terrorist acts, and that was just for starters. The Internal Revenue Service was crawling in and out of his records, giving his financial history a proctological exam. He knew they'd find more than ample discrepancies to build a case that would make Al Capone look innocent by comparison.

The link to Trogg was thrice damning, because with it came complicity in all of Trogg's murderous crimes, including the assault on the *Hard Times*. They hadn't uncovered his direct hand in those events, but they would. It seemed Commander Heaney had come down with a bad case of guilty conscience and had offered to testify in exchange for leniency. On hearing that, the chief of police had put the barrel of a .38 in his mouth and spread his brains all over the inside of his unmarked car.

The only good news was that the vigilante—the man who'd done so much damage to the Purists, the man who'd come looking for him in his office just as the man *mistaken* for him had brought Kohler's world crashing down around him—had failed to take his revenge. Kohler was still alive.

He was still trying to decide how he felt about that.

In his shirtsleeves, deprived of his belt and his shoelaces, treated like a common criminal, sitting in an interrogation room—the indignity, the ignominy of it, galled him and shamed him.

The big man in black opened the door, secured it behind him and sat down across the table from Kohler.

"Cooper," the man said. "I'm with the Justice Department."

"So I'm told," Kohler said, uninterested.

"You're going to tell me everything I want to know. I know you're holding things back. You need to tell me everything."

"And if I don't?" Keeler asked.

The man from Justice stared at him, his gaze boring into Kohler.

"You will."

GARY ROOK WAS BACK IN hell.

He swam through the netherworld that was unconsciousness, tortured by visions of Jennifer and dreams of his failed revenge. Trogg, Kohler, most of the

Purists—all his hard work and all that death, all those bloody days and nights, had ended in failure. Jennifer's spirit screamed at him from a place beyond death. Rook had nothing to tell her, could do nothing to appease her.

Gary Rook's comatose body lay in a hospital bed, in a private room guarded by a single police officer. One of Rook's arms bore an IV and a monitoring electrode. The other was handcuffed to the railing of the bed, an action that had brought no small number of protests from the hospital staff. Bolan had insisted and the officers who'd been to Rook's crime scenes were inclined to agree. The man would probably never wake up, but if he did, he was much better off chained up.

The room was devoid of decorations, utilitarian and antiseptic in form and function. The lighting was kept dim, the curtains drawn. Beyond those curtains, the single window was barred.

For Gary Rook, there was no escape—not in the world of the living, and not from the dead.

Stony Man Farm, Virginia

BARBARA PRICE BRUSHED a lock of honey-blond hair from her face and sat in a chair next to Aaron Kurtzman's wheelchair.

Bolan had contacted them and filled them in on the developments in Syracuse, including Grimaldi's last-minute elimination of a sniper. The locals had managed to take some prints from the dead shooter and copies had been passed on to the Farm, as well as complete files on Trogg Sharpe, his dead accomplices and Roger

Kohler. The rap sheets on some of the dead gang members were a sight to behold. The fact that they had all been walking about instead of behind bars was a sad commentary on the state of the American justice system.

Coordinating the surveillance data from the Department of Homeland Security, disturbing questions had been raised. Analysis of Roger Kohler's phone calls had turned up a link to a third party, who from all indications was an agent of a foreign government. Price had her theories, as did Kurtzman. Price watched as the computer expert dug through everything he could find on Kohler, trying to find a connection. Bank statements, computer records, trips abroad, known associates—Kurtzman was digging through it all, widening his search to include the records, travel and electronic trails generated by those associates and then *their* associates.

If the transcripts were any indication, they did not have much time. They had to find the link fast. To whom and to what had Kohler been beholden? What plans were afoot?

Grim but determined, Kurtzman plowed through the data.

Ithaca, New York

ZHONGCHAO HU ROSE TO leave his office, late for a meeting with the admissions department. He found Nick Kaplewski from the information technology department blocking his way.

"Nick," Hu greeted him, his accent still thick despite

twenty years of English fluency. "I have an appointment right now. Can you stop by later?"

"No," Kaplewski told him, refusing to move. Hu was brought up short. He looked up at the man who towered over him.

Kaplewski was young, but good at his job. Barely out of college himself, he had already made a notable reputation. As the IT coordinator he was responsible for all of the college's computer systems—and for the elaborate programs that tracked and logged activity in order to keep the college and its students out of legal trouble. Kaplewski had spearheaded the blocking of file sharing programs, preventing the use of the college's network for accessing such sites.

Kaplewski was lean, broad-shouldered and intense. His naturally curly, dark hair was cropped close to his skull. Dressed casually—he was indistinguishable from the student body, most days—he nevertheless managed to project authority. Hu had interacted with Kaplewski favorably a few times in the course of administrative work, but he had never seen the young man look so agitated.

"What do you want?" Hu demanded.

"We need to talk about your e-mails and uploads," Kaplewski said.

"What do you mean?"

"Don't play dumb, Mr. Hu," Kaplewski said, shouldering his way into the room and forcing Hu to move back. "I've been tracking your file transfers and your e-mail for months. We aren't talking about simple violations of administrative policy, either. I'm seriously considering getting in touch with the Secret Service, or whoever gets alerted for stuff like this."

"I'm sure I don't know what you're talking about," Hu said, stalling.

"I'm sure you do," Kaplewski told him. "Did you think you could trade e-mails with mainland China without raising suspicion in any way? Did you think you could upload schematics of the campus layout, or files detailing campus security and public safety patrols, and no one would think that odd? Do you have any idea just how much monitoring of our system is performed by the government?"

"You exaggerate," Hu told him. "The government does not have that kind of access."

"You only think it doesn't," Kaplewski informed him. "Tell me what you've got going on, Mr. Hu. Convince me this isn't a national security matter. I'm not stupid. I know the difference between illegally downloading movies and transmitting sensitive information to a foreign government."

"This...this is a mistake," Hu sputtered. "I have done nothing of the kind. Nick, how many years have I worked here? How many alumni weekends have I attended? I was on staff here when you were a student here. You cannot believe I would do such things."

"Can't I?" Kaplewski asked. "The files don't lie."

"I do not dispute that the data you have tracked was sent," Hu said, "but it was not me."

"No one has access to your terminal and your account but you."

"You are not so naive," Hu told him. "There are

hackers. There are students playing pranks. There are racists. American sentiment toward my former government is not exactly positive. Americans believe the People's Republic of China is an evil empire bent on world domination and threatening the United States."

Kaplewski scoffed. "I'm not political," he said, "and I'm not a racist. What I do know is that I'm in charge of watching for just this kind of threat. Damn it, Mr. Hu, I'd rather have found you downloading pornography or something. This is *serious.*"

"Yes, it is serious," Hu agreed. "Please, Nick, you must help me. I am innocent. You must help me find how this was done."

Kaplewski looked dubious. "You're serious? You really didn't send those files? Tell me now, if you did."

"No, no," Hu insisted. "I could never do such a thing. I love America. I love my job here. I love Ithaca. I am no traitor. I would never endanger this campus, or any of its students. I have been targeted. It is a prank, or something more sinister. I did not do this thing."

Kaplewski looked ready to accept the idea. Hu pressed. "Perhaps someone has found a way to access my terminal when I am not here, or even when I am."

"That's not supposed to be possible," Kaplewski said thoughtfully. "I suppose if they linked to the router physically—let me take a look."

"Yes, yes, please do," Hu said, moving out of the way. Kaplewski moved behind the desk and crawled under it, removing a penlight from his pocket. He began searching behind the computer, which sat on the floor under the desk.

Hu glanced around. He quietly closed the glass door to his office. Administrators moved about in the corridor and the other offices. He would have to act quickly and quietly.

Waiting until there was no one outside in the hallway, Hu grabbed the mouse from his desk. He yanked and the mouse pulled free from behind the computer.

"Hey," Kaplewski said from under the desk. "Did you just yank that mouse out?"

Hu walked briskly behind the desk, curling the mouse cord into both of his hands. As Kaplewski started to back out from under the desk, Hu bent over him and looped the mouse cord over his neck. He yanked back and up with all his might, twisting the cord to tighten it more deeply in the young man's throat.

Kaplewski's eyes bulged and he began frantically tearing at the cord, unable to get his fingers under it. He made hoarse choking sounds, unable to draw or expel air, unable to shout or call for help. Desperately he fought, slamming Hu painfully into the corner of the desk, but he could not dislodge the smaller man. Finally, his face turning red, sweat pouring from his forehead, he dropped to his knees. His fingernails drew blood from his own neck as he tried in vain to pull the cord free. Hu put all his weight on the cord, sliding to the floor behind Kaplewski's back, dragging the man down with him.

Finally, mercifully, Kaplewski stopped struggling.

Hu maintained the pressure for a full thirty seconds more before rising. There was still no one in the corridor. Quickly he pushed Kaplewski's body under the desk. Moments later, Brenda Carstairs stopped and knocked on his door.

Brenda was a pretty young redhead with porcelain skin and large, hazel-blue eyes. She was Hu's assistant events coordinator.

"Zhong?" she said, opening the door halfway. "You okay in here?"

Flushed, Hu looked up at her. "Exercises," he said. "My doctor tells me my heart needs more aerobic exercise."

"Don't you do Tai Chi, or something like that?" Brenda asked him.

"Yes, but it is not strenuous enough, the doctor claims."

Brenda nodded. "You sure you're okay? You look like you're not feeling well."

"I will be all right," Hu said.

"Well, don't overdo it," Brenda told him. She closed the door and continued down the hall.

Hu looked down at the body under the desk.

Somehow, he would have to remove it without anyone noticing. Then he would have to see if there was some way to cover his tracks in the IT department. Like it or not, he was committed now. His dreams of living out his days in the United States were over. He would have no choice but to return to China when his work was finished.

He would have to be careful. If he failed, Chang would see to it that he did not live to go back.

Syracuse, New York

LYNN STANZA WALKED briskly through the foyer of the Public Safety building, her heels clicking on the polished floor. She wore an impeccably tailored gray designer suit. Her straight bottle-blond hair, which reached to the middle of her back, was freshly styled and perfect. Her eyes were partially hidden behind over-size designer sunglasses. She stood just over six feet tall. As she passed, many of the officers present turned to look—and those who knew who she was shook their heads in disgust.

She strode to the main desk and removed her glasses, eyeing the desk sergeant imperiously.

"Yes?" he said.

"Lynn Stanza, counsel for Roger Kohler," she informed him. "You have thirty seconds to put me in the same room with my client or you'll be a rent-a-cop at Carousel Mall by the time I'm finished with you."

Stanza was well-known to the Syracuse police and to the local criminal element—at least, the high-paid criminal element. A partner in the firm of Reich, Stanza and Hirsch, she had kept Roger Kohler and a slew of other wealthy clients one step ahead of the law for almost a decade. In Syracuse, in a small pond where even the weaker fish were still predators, Stanza was a shark. She knew it, her clients knew it and the Onon-daga County District Attorney's Office knew it. No one gave her any trouble as she was ushered into Kohler's presence.

Kohler was seated in the interrogation room across from another man. Stanza gave the tall, dark-haired man the once-over. He stood and she raised her apprai-sal of him; he moved like a panther. An electric thrill went through her as her eyes walked up and down his body. He stared her down as if he would snap her neck as soon as look at her, which only made her more interested.

"Lynn Stanza," she said by rote, "counsel for Roger Kohler. And you are?"

"Cooper," he said. "Justice Department."

"Mr. Cooper," Stanza told him, "my client will not be answering your questions without legal counsel."

"Fine," he agreed. "You can stay. Your client has a lot to answer for."

"That won't be happening," she said, cocking one hip as she looked him over again. "Mr. Kohler will be leaving with me. I think if you'll check you'll find that Judge Morley has agreed to bail and that the bail has been paid."

"Just how was this arranged?" he asked her.

"That's not your concern," she told him, removing the appropriate documentation from within her suit jacket and slapping it down on the metal table.

"Roger, I'm sure you've had quite enough of Mr. Cooper's hospitality. Would you care to leave?"

"Absolutely," Kohler said, standing and smoothing his clothes. Already a hint of his old swagger was back. The Executioner was forced to look on as the pair walked out without further comment.

10

Ithaca, New York

Chang, his bodyguards in tow, swept through the rooms of the safehouse, surveying the supplies laid in by his men. On a cluttered table in the living room, and on the walls surrounding it, printouts of the layout of the Ithaca College campus were pinned up or spread out, highlighted and marked as needed. A complete itinerary for the day in question, two weeks hence, was included. Zhongchao Hu had proved his worth several times, Chang reflected. It would be a pity when the time came to kill him.

No doubt the poor fool pictured himself returning home, a hero of the people. Well, he would have to settle for being a martyr of the people. Chang could take no chances—all involved in the project would have to be silenced. Given what they had overheard, even his own bodyguards would be terminated eventually. He would wait to do that, however. It wouldn't do to have them eliminated prematurely, especially before they knew how successful the plan had been.

In cardboard boxes, plastic jugs and larger plastic drums, the chemical supplies they would need were stacked haphazardly throughout the safehouse. Except for the table and three wooden chairs around it, the house was devoid of furniture. All available space had been devoted to storing the chemicals and other elements that they required.

All that remained now was the methamphetamine.

Chang had followed the news of Kohler's arrest and the capture of another man believed responsible for several violent murders in the central New York area. No doubt the man was the "problem" Kohler had tried to so hard to solve, the problem that had destroyed his supply of the drugs in the first place. Without the corrupt American, Chang would have to call on other suppliers. It was critical that the suppliers be of domestic origin. It was the whole purpose of the attack.

Only an event on the scale of September 11—a traumatic event about which the Americans could wail and gnash their teeth for the next half a decade—would suffice. When they realized it came from within their own ranks, they would begin to tear themselves apart. Chang and those like him, those tasked by their government with conducting operations like these, would continue to hasten the rot of the American redwood from within. The Americans saw themselves as invincible and righteous. They would learn they were neither. They would come to hate themselves. Weakened, they would fall—on their own, or at the hands of the ever-growing People's Liberation Army, when the time came.

Lost in thought, Chang almost did not hear his phone ring. He removed it delicately from his pocket, flipped it open and put it to his ear.

"Yes?"

"Chang, it's Kohler."

"Yes," Chang said, surprised. "I confess I did not expect to hear from you again."

"I realize it has been a mess," Kohler said, "but I can still provide the trade goods we discussed. If you pay me in cash, rather than the negotiable bonds on which we agreed, I will give you the product for twenty-five percent less. I can't haggle, Comrade Chang. That deal should be more than good enough for both of us."

Chang paused, genuinely interested. "But…what of your *financial constraints?*"

"Those constraints have changed," Kohler admitted.

Indeed they have, Chang thought. *No doubt you seek the liquid funds to allow you to flee the country.* Aloud, he told Kohler, "Go on, Mr. Kohler. Tell me about the trade goods and when I can expect to receive them."

Syracuse, New York

OFFICER PAGLIA AND HIS partner, Harold "Rizzo" Rizzoli, stopped at the secure nurse's station. They'd been diverted from their usual route near the hospital to check in on Gary Rook's status, at the behest of the deputy chief of police. The DCP was understandably nervous, given the burgeoning scandal developing around SWAT Commander Heaney, the chief of police, the recent terrorist attack in Clinton Square and the vigilante killings involving Rook.

Both Paglia and Rizzoli were relatively young, but where Paglia was of average size, even slight of build, Rizzoli was a tank. He lifted weights and followed a strict healthly diet. He'd won the department's annual "strong man" competition two years running. With his huge chest and overbuilt arms, he walked like a gorilla. Officers who did not know him tended to dismiss Rizzo as a no-necked, brainless oaf, but Paglia knew better. The man was fiercely loyal, had a relatively innocent disposition and bore almost no one ill will. He was not someone you wanted to box or wrestle, however, and more than a few unruly suspects had discovered that he was not the cop at whom to swing.

"Officers Paglia and Rizzoli to see suspect Gary Rook," Paglia told the nurse on duty.

"Room 376," she said, gesturing down the hallway.

With Rizzoli hulking alongside, Paglia made his way down the hall. As they neared the room, however, Paglia stopped his partner, placing a hand against the bigger man's chest. "Wait a minute, Rizzo," he said. "Where's the officer on duty?"

The chair in front of the secure hospital room was empty.

"Call it in," Paglia said, drawing his gun. He approached the door cautiously and, standing to one side, reached out to grasp the handle. Behind him, Rizzoli spoke quietly but succinctly into the handset clipped to the epaulet of his uniform shirt.

Paglia whipped the door open, covering the opening with his handgun.

There was no one inside.

Paglia took one step into the room. Too late, he caught movement from the corner of his eye. The inert form of Officer Saul Moyers collided with him, knocking him to the ground. He struck his head and the world went blurry.

Gary Rook plunged from his room, the side railing from his hospital bed still handcuffed to his wrist. Rizzoli had a fleeting impression of the twisted end of that railing, where Rook had to have ripped it free, as the railing whistled through the air and struck him in the face. He went down hard, grunting.

Rook was on top of him, battering down with the railing, using it like a club. Rizzoli raised one beefy arm to ward off the psychotic ex-Marine, then surged to his feet. He rammed Rook backward, hammering the man once, then twice, with his calloused fists. In his college days, Rizzoli had broken more than a few knuckles in fraternity brawls. He resorted to instinct and brute force now as then, stumbling over the prone form of his partner as he fought Rook to the floor. He had a chance. He could win.

He almost managed it.

He had straddled Rook's chest and began to pummel his face, his sidearm forgotten, when Rook caught him on the side of the head with the corner of the bed railing. Concussed, Rizzoli dropped heavily, the impact echoing through the off-white room.

The last thing he felt, before losing consciousness, was Rook groping for the handcuff keys on the cop's belt.

Stony Man Farm, Virginia

AARON KURTZMAN'S FINGERS flew over the keyboard as he continued sleuthing, poking, prodding and processing the mountain of data concerning Roger Kohler. At the adjoining workstation, Akira Tokaido, recalled from leave to assist, hunkered over his own screens. The young Asian man wore earbuds, and Kurtzman could hear the heavy metal music seeping out. He wondered, for the thousandth time, how the young man managed to avoid incurring permanent hearing loss from the constant noise.

Tokaido had been connecting some data links found in Kohler's interaction with overseas firms and personnel. He looked up at one point, switched off his music and turned to eye the larger man.

"Bear," he said, "I think I have something."

Kurtzman wheeled over to the workstation. "What?"

"You said Kohler was involved in running crystal meth, right?"

"He was using gang muscle to produce and move it, yeah," Kurtzman verified. "He was brokering a sale of a large quantity of it. That much we know. I'm trying to backtrace that contact. We think they front for another country, maybe the Chinese or a Middle East nation."

"I've found something unusual here," he said. "It's a bulletin board posting originating from Ithaca College, New York."

"That's near where Striker is operating," Kurtzman said. "Ithaca is an hour south of Syracuse."

"This posting," Tokaido said, pointing to the screen, "is supposedly the manifesto of a group calling itself the North American Liberation Group, a Christian Identity sect. It's pretty rambling, but at its heart is a description of a chemical weapon—specifically, how to make it."

"Sounds like the usual crackpot nonsense," Kurtzman commented.

"It might," Tokaido admitted, "except that this is a formula for a home-brewed nerve gas. It's pretty unusual, but the long and the short of it is that when airborne and inhaled in sufficient concentration, it speeds up the victim's heart rate until the heart almost literally explodes."

"And?" Kurtzman asked.

"A key component to the formula is methamphetamine," Tokaido said.

Kurtzman got very interested very quickly. "So the link we're looking for might be a domestic terrorist group, some kind of White Supremacy, antigovernment thing?"

"That is what we are *meant* to believe, I think," Tokaido told him. "I checked. The group has a Web site, referenced in the post. It says exactly what you'd expect from such a group—Big Brother is watching, we must secure a future for white children, the mud races are overrunning us, the liberal politicians are in cahoots with the one-world Zionist-run government, blah, blah, blah. But the Web site was only registered last week, using an anonymous and supposedly untraceable Web host."

"Does that prove anything?"

"Not by itself, no," Tokaido said. "But the bulletin board posting hasn't actually been posted yet. Our computers turned it up because, through Department of Homeland Security, we can search things not accessible to the public, behind the firewalls of the networks involved. This post is dated two weeks from now. It's specifically planned for then and not before."

"And?" Kurtzman pressed.

"And," Tokaido said, allowing himself a self-satisfied smile, "anonymous and untraceable rarely is on the Internet, at least when we're behind the machines doing the tracing. The Web host is bounced through a couple of anonymous servers and routers, but the source is actually mainland China."

"China…" Kurtzman considered it.

"There's more," Tokaido told him. "Two weeks from now, Ithaca College is slated to host a very important guest speaker. She is the freshman senator from New York State."

Kurtzman stared at the screen for another moment. Then his hand shot for the nearest phone.

ZHONGCHAO HU SAT at his desk, sweating.

It had been a very difficult morning. The night before, he had waited until everyone else had gone home for the evening. It had been nearly 7:00 p.m. before Brenda stopped by to wish him goodnight. He had waited another half hour to be sure, all the while near hysteria because he could not remember which days of the week the cleaning service came in to vacuum and dust the offices. Finally, using a cart he borrowed from the copier room and covered with several copies of the *Ithaca Times,* he had managed to drag Nick Kaplewski's soiled corpse through the halls of the administration building, down one floor in the elevator and into a Dumpster behind the building. He prayed no one thought to check the Dumpster before it was emptied into a truck at the end of the week. He had covered the body with as much other refuse as he could find. Now all he could do was wait.

He had to maintain his cover until the Senator arrived for the Political Science Forum. The event was a big one, as this was the most prestigious guest the college had hosted since a former President had offered a commencement address some years before. Tickets had been strictly doled out according to the administration's rules, and the college auditorium would be standing room only. Several state legislators were expected to be on hand, as well, though there was some debate as to whether the governor would make an appearance. Even without him, the auditorium would host a powerful chunk of New York's political might, as well as a capacity crowd of young, impressionable college students.

When Chang's people released the nerve gas, they would all die, horribly—and the press coverage for the event would ensure that their grisly deaths were televised. The recordings of the event would be played again and again in the domestic and international media. It would be a telling blow against the Americans, to be sure.

Hu had been instructed to see to it that the domestic terrorism link was made, and from the very college where the attack took place. He did not believe Kaplewski had found the timed bulletin board posting, which Hu had arranged during a surreptitious visit to the IT center. That the young man had managed to track Hu's other activity disturbed him and was a testament to Kaplewski's skill. Hu thought he had taken sufficient precautions. Still, he would double-check. He had to make sure the posting went live after the event and that the Web site it linked to was fully prepared. The text of both would be analyzed and processed and rehashed, again and again, as the nonstop media cycle mashed and regurgitated it, looking for new meaning where none was to be found. It was vital that the Americans believe it to be genuine, that they focus inward and not abroad when they sought a target for their wrath.

The sleeping giant was about to eat itself. Hu knew that there was a time when he would have relished the prospect. Now, he felt nothing. He hoped only that he would warm to the idea once he was on a plane back to China.

Syracuse, New York

ROOK, HIS BRAIN STILL fogged from his injuries, did his best to walk casually, his stolen Syracuse police uniform ill-fitting but at least large enough to cover his big frame. When he'd opened his eyes to find himself still alive and chained to the hospital bed, he'd paused only long enough to gather his strength. Then he'd worked at the railing until he was sure he could snap it, called weakly for help and ambushed his guard. It was bad luck that the two other cops had shown up just when they had—but also fortunate, for Rook. He'd taken the big one's clothes and .40-caliber pistols from both men. The smaller one had been carrying a Ka-Bar TDI knife, too, which Rook had gladly placed on his own belt. The little pistol-gripped knife was razor-sharp and made up for in blade shape and edge geometry what it lacked in overall length.

After running from the secure ward, pausing to cut the duty nurse's throat, Rook found a supply closet where he changed. The hospital alarm was only just sounding when he walked off the grounds, trying to appear casual, hoping the cuts and bruises on his face were not too obvious. He had chosen a direction and started walking, heading north out of downtown.

He felt nauseous and cotton-mouthed. His head ached as if it would split open. He needed food and something to drink, he supposed, but he doubted he could keep either down.

One of his stolen pistols was holstered at his side, while the other was tucked behind his belt at the small of his back. The knife was on his support side, where he could draw it as easily as a pistol. A couple of drivers passing him on the street waved, and Rook had absently waved back. He supposed he did look the part, though he hoped no one would examine him too closely.

Worse than the aches and pains racking his body was the thought that he had failed.

The leader of the Purists was dead. The man behind them, Roger Kohler, had been arrested and was beyond his reach. Short of mounting an assault on the Public Safety building, assuming Kohler was even still there, Rook could think of no way to get to the man. He considered attacking the cops and fighting his way to Kohler, but even he had to admit that such a plan was far-fetched. They would cut him down long before he reached his goal, and he would be back where he started. Jennifer would remain unavenged, and Rook would have no more opportunities.

The Purists were gone or, if any survived, they had fled the area. The commando had finished the work Rook had begun. The big man had been more than a match for him, too, though Rook was confident he could eventually take the other soldier if he had to. They were so much alike, he thought. Why could the other man not see what needed to be done? He had spoken of understanding, of loss and vengeance. They were empty words if the commando could not see how wrong Jennifer's fate had been, how those responsible had to pay.

How could he make the man see? How could he make *everyone* see? If Jennifer was to have justice, the world had to know what had happened to her and why. Syracuse and countless cities like it would have to learn the lesson Rook had learned so painfully.

11

Cortland, New York

Chang sat in the back of the Mercedes, his coat pooled around him, smoking a cigarette. His bodyguards sat in front, one of them behind the wheel. Chang sometimes wondered what it was they thought about, sitting silently for hours, awaiting his bidding and ready at all times to take a bullet to save his life. Did they get bored? Did they ever consider finding other employment? It amused him to ponder it.

They sat in the parking lot of a chain restaurant, part of a larger plaza that included a number of stores and a bank. Chang watched the mall's sign alternate between an incorrect gauge of the outside temperature and an inaccurate accounting of the time of day.

The bodyguards stirred when the rear driver's-side door opened. A slim man of middle age and medium build, his brown hair receding from the front, sat down without invitation. He wore wire-framed glasses, a prim blue suit and a yellow bow tie. His features were, at first glance, pleasant. When he fixed his gaze on Chang, the genial illusion was dispelled. The man had the eyes of a predator.

"Mr. Matthews," Chang acknowledged.

Aaron Matthews nodded. He had a slim leather briefcase with him, which he propped on his knees. He opened it and turned it so that Chang could see the contents. Within the file folders it contained were several photographs and stacks of notes.

"As you requested," Matthews said, "I have complete dossiers, including backdated passports, birth certificates and records of employment, all of which have been inserted in multiple computer networks. These men did not exist before last week. Now they have credit ratings, military service, the occasional dishonorable discharge from that service, and other hallmarks of the living. Their identities are yours to do with what you will."

"You are not at all curious as to why I wished these?" Chang asked.

"Mr. Chang," Matthews told him, "please do not insult me. I am not an amateur. I have been performing this service for two decades. I am still alive and free because I absolutely never ask questions of that type. After I leave this vehicle, you will never see me again and I will have forgotten you exist."

Chang nodded, once, very faintly. The bodyguard in the passenger seat shifted slightly. Chang fancied that he could hear the safety of the guard's pistol being engaged but knew that was largely his imagination.

"I cannot argue with that," Chang told him. He removed an envelope from within his suit jacket and handed it to the man.

Glancing within the envelope, Matthews nodded once and then exited the vehicle. Chang watched him go, considered shooting him in the back, then dismissed the thought. There was a man with whom they would have no trouble in the future. He glanced down for a moment and, when he returned his gaze to the window, Matthews was nowhere to be seen.

Chang sat back in the leather upholstery of the Mercedes, removed another cigarette from his silver cigarette case and fired it with his custom silver-plated cigarette lighter, all the while pondering the evils of materialism.

He held in his hand the records of men who did not exist—but who would be believed to exist. They were the perfect shadow force, a domestic terrorist group who could never be killed, never apprehended, never stopped. Their strikes would chill the American people and their resilience would rally the nation's enemies. Law-enforcement officials, even the President and his lackeys, would talk tough into television cameras for the benefit of the proletariat under their fat thumbs. Then they would fail, and continue to fail, and ultimately look like the fools that they were, when their threats and their posturing produced no arrests and no dead terrorists.

Chang's people would continue behind the scenes, wreaking havoc. It would start with the nerve gas attack at the college, an attack that would shake America's faith in itself. It would continue with larger and still larger strikes, all of them cleverly disguised as domestic crimes of the most horrible magnitude.

The thought brought a smile to Chang's lips. He was about to signal the guard in the driver's seat to take them back to Ithaca when his phone rang.

"Yes?" Chang answered, knowing it would be Kohler.

"All is arranged," Kohler informed him. "The product sample will be delivered to your field office today. They've been brought in at great expense overnight. You will be pleased with the quality."

"I had better be," Chang said, enjoying Kohler's discomfort on the phone. With the knowledge that his phone calls could be and had been monitored, Kohler had taken to engaging in verbal gymnastics over the open line. Chang himself was a nonentity, as far as the United States authorities knew. He could come and go as he pleased. He was confident that his identity and his activities were buried deeply enough behind virtual firewalls that no one could ferret him out.

"I look forward to establishing the factory in Hong Kong," Kohler said irrelevantly. Chang almost barked a laugh as he hung up.

"Go," he said, kicking the driver's seat with his left foot. "Take us to the safehouse."

Stony Man Farm, Virginia

AKIRA TOKAIDO WAS digging deeply into the virtual firewalls protecting Roger Kohler's foreign contacts, searching for the identity of the mysterious individual with whom Kohler had been plotting. To do so had been no small feat; it had required the efforts of both Tokaido and Kurtzman working around the clock, spelling each other off as they hacked their way through layers of security, programming traps and misinformation.

Finally, they had uncovered a man who was not supposed to exist—General Cao Chang, rumored to be a high-level functionary in Chinese special operations and reported as deceased, sometimes violently so, no less than six separate times in the last twenty years. Firm biographical information was hard to come by, but it was clear that Chang was an experienced and ruthless operative. If any man was capable of coordinating or even conducting an operation of the type they suspected was being undertaken, it was Chang. The data trails had finally led Tokaido to a holding company to which Chang had been linked several times. The holding company owned three properties in Ithaca: a parking garage and an office building in downtown Ithaca—and a house in a residential district not far from the other two properties.

Barbara Price looked on as Tokaido explained what he'd found and how he found it. Kurtzman grunted and Price nodded. This was it; this was what they'd been trying to find.

Price picked up the phone and dialed Bolan's number.

BOLAN WAS SITTING AT Larry Kearney's kitchen table, drinking coffee, as the man finished relating another story of his early journalist days.

His secure phone rang quietly. He took it out, snapped it open and placed it to his ear. After a moment he nodded for Kearney's benefit and then listened some more. "Okay," he acknowledged when Price was finished. "That has to be it. I'm on my way now." He closed the phone, pocketed it and stood.

"Don't get up," he told Kearney.

"The hell you say," Kearney scoffed, pushing himself to his feet, using the table for leverage. He offered one big paw and took Bolan's hand in a near bone-crushing grip, grinning from ear to ear. "Let me say, sir, that it has been a distinct pleasure."

"If getting choked half to death is your idea of a pleasure, I'd hate to see what you consider a bad day," Bolan told him.

"Well, it's all relative." Kearney chuckled. "You tell Hal I'm damned grateful for everything. If he owed me any favors, well, come to think of it, he owed me a lot of favors, but I'd say you paid them all off."

"I'll tell him," Bolan promised. "Take care of yourself."

"You, too, soldier," Kearney said.

The Executioner left Kearney's home and walked to his rented SUV. When he was seated inside, he called Jack Grimaldi.

"We're a go," Bolan told him. He gave the Stony Man pilot the coordinates Price had given him, which corresponded to the address of the safehouse linked to General Cao Chang. He also passed on the synopsis of the nerve gas plan Tokaido and Kurtzman had uncovered. Though some of it was still conjecture at this point, it rang true and made perfect sense. He would go to the safehouse, find all the evidence he needed to seal Chang's fate, and then see to it that the Chinese operative never got the chance to deploy his phony domestic terrorism.

The SUV surged away from the curve with the Executioner behind the wheel.

ROGER KOHLER, WEARING slacks but barefoot and shirtless, sat on the edge of the bed in the master bedroom of the condominium he maintained. The furnishings in the spacious unit were unremarkable. Kohler had ordered them from a catalog and hired a designer to see to their disposition, but he did not much care. He had spent far more time choosing the dark, masculine furniture in his office than he had bothered wasting on a place like this.

Kohler watched the large plasma television nervously as Lynn Stanza gave an interview to the local press, asserting Kohler's innocence and disparaging the heavy-handed brutality of the Syracuse police. They were, Stanza asserted on his behalf, entirely too consumed with persecuting a legitimate businessman, perhaps out of a sense of envy. Kohler wished he shared the confidence the woman projected in declaring the outcome of Kohler's trial before it had begun. Not for the first time in the last half hour did he consider liquidating his assets and fleeing the country.

He could afford to wait. There was still time to take that option, if the trial went badly. Stanza could keep the courts tied up and the police confounded for as long as he needed, if not indefinitely. Part of him had always wanted to invite Stanza to the condominium, but he had a strict policy when it came to mingling business with pleasure. That was the only reason he had never bullied Lori into bed with him, no matter how good she looked behind the desk in front of his office.

At least Chang would have his shipment by now, freeing Kohler of that particular worry. He could not afford to make enemies of the Chinese. Once they had transferred the money into his account, he would feel much better. There was the very real possibility that they would renege on the deal. Kohler had no leverage, no means to strike back if they chose to screw him. With Trogg and the Purists dead, his ability to affect change in the criminal element was effectively eliminated. While Abbot could perform wet work, sending a single loyal bodyguard against the Chinese syndicate and the Communist government backing it seemed like a poor proposition.

It occurred to Kohler, then, that Abbot had not checked in for more than an hour, which was unlike him.

Kohler rose and padded down the half flight of stairs leading from the bedroom to the great room. As he crossed the room, the sliding glass doors leading to the condominium's small balcony shattered inward. Abbot fell to the floor in a bloody heap, covered in glass and staring blankly at the ceiling. The plain rosewood handle of a dagger projected from the man's left eye. His throat was also cut from ear to ear.

Kohler ran. He bounded up the half flight of stairs and slammed the bedroom door behind him, throwing the bolt. As he did so he felt the door shudder under the violent impact of a kick thrown by his pursuer. Abbot's murderer wasted no words and no time, throwing himself against the door.

Dropping to his knees by the bed, Kohler ducked his hand underneath it to tap the four-button electronic combination on the handgun safe he kept there. He removed a Heckler & Koch USP Compact .45 with a stainless-steel slide. Racking the chamber in his fight-or-flight state, he barely processed the live round flying over his sholder. The weapon still had seven rounds in it as he leveled it at the door and fired the weapon until the slide locked back.

Breathing heavily, he stared at the door in the sudden silence.

Nothing.

He stumbled backward and fumbled in the safe for the spare loaded magazine he kept there. Reloading, he crept toward the door, cautiously pulling it open as he peered out of the room. When he saw no one, he took a step out.

Strong hands grabbed and pulled, sending him head over heels down the stairs. The gun flew out of his hand as he lost his grip.

Something snapped. His reflexes took over. Kohler rolled and sprang up on the balls of his bare feet, his hands extended before him, his body tensed as he faced the threat.

The Asian man who faced him looked slightly amused. He wore loose black clothing that was not quite casual wear but stopped short of being BDUs. He looked like a Vietcong guerrilla. On his belt was an empty sheath that had, no doubt, held the knife now buried in Abbot's brain.

He was otherwise unarmed.

"Who are you?" Kohler demanded.

"You may call me Song," the Asian man told him. "I am here to remove you."

"But why?" Kohler asked, confused. "I've upheld my end of the deal. I've provided the product—the *meth*—that Chang said he needed. How have I offended the Chinese government? Or is this personal? Did Chang decide to take me out on his own?"

"He did not," Song said. "You are a liability, Kohler. It is that simple."

"But why?"

"You will figure it out eventually, I imagine," Song said, pretending to examine the fingernails of his right hand. "That is why you cannot be permitted to live."

Song struck. He lashed out with a vicious low-line kick, entering and firing a series of chain punches, hammering Kohler's ribs. The much larger man reflexively threw a lateral elbow at Song, catching the man in the side of the head and sending him reeling back.

"So," Song said. "You are not simply a businessman who lifts weights."

"I'm going to fucking kill you," Kohler snarled, his rage and frustration welling up to consume him. Finally, he had a target for his anxiety, a single human being on whom to vent his outrage at what had befallen him. He was going to take great pleasure breaking Song's bones before slowly squeezing the life out of him.

Kohler went on the offensive. He struck with a flurry of ridge-hands and edge-of-hand blows, following up with roundhouse kicks and front kicks, kneeing as he closed the distance. Song dodged or blocked with little difficulty, one step ahead of the bigger man, faster and more comfortable working the low line as he chopped away at Kohler's foundation. Kohler quickly recognized Song's fighting style as Wing Chun Kung Fu. He knew it emphasized infighting and worked well for a man of Song's stature, who could not simply muscle through his techniques to overpower a man of Kohler's size. Pleased to have something physical to do, Kohler did his best to keep Song out of range.

Kohler lashed out with long-range kicks, scoring one good blow on Song's knee before the smaller man fooled him. He performed a half-jumping kick that Kohler at first took to be a high-line snap—before he remembered that such kicks were not performed in Wing Chun. He realized Song was using the maneuver to enter, closing to infighting distance and driving a vicious knee into Kohler's midsection. Then he rained elbows on Kohler's back, hammering the man to the floor.

Kohler shot for Song's legs, dragging him down. Wing Chun fighters were notoriously weak as grapplers, while Kohler's training had included groundwork. He struggled for position and managed to mount the smaller man, preparing to fire punches into Song's head. He cocked his fist back, his technique gone, his rage all-consuming—

From a second sheath at his back, Song drew a dagger identical to the one in Abbot's head, driving it deeply into Kohler's flank and twisting it viciously. Kohler felt nothing, then an icy numbness that spread from the tip of the knife—then pain. He gasped and could not resist as Song tossed him to the side, where he landed heavily on his stomach, clutching dumbly at the wound. Song rose quickly to his feet to stand over his vanquished foe.

"An invigorating match," Song told the flailing Kohler, watching as blood soaked the plush carpet. "One grows tired of simply pulling triggers and longs for a contest between men. You did well."

Kohler stared up at him, uncomprehending.

Song raised his foot and brought it down, the ax kick driving the heel of his shoe between Kohler's eyes.

12

Ithaca, New York

Mark Margray poked his head into Nick Kaplewski's main work area, a pair of tables bearing multiple monitors and servers at the rear of the college's main computer lab. Margray, an engineer on loan from a local technology company, had been working with Kaplewski to set up a next-generation synchronized network for the college. They had done well together, making real progress, but there was much work to be done on the server they were building more or less from scratch. Kaplewski had missed their scheduled meeting in the lab, but that was not unusual. Margray had simply written it off and come back later, wondering if Kaplewski would have a tale to tell of meeting some pretty coed and taking her back to his place.

Margray was surprised, as he entered the lab, to find Zhongchao Hu working at one of Kaplewski's terminals. As far as he knew, the man had no reason to be there and was no more than a passing acquaintance to Kaplewski.

"What are you doing here?" he asked bluntly.

Hu looked him over as if sizing him up. The two men were the same height, but Margray was much stockier, with a thick chest and the rolling gait of a man who knew how to throw a barroom haymaker. He wore jeans and a flannel shirt over a T-shirt, his chest hair poking up over the neckline.

"I'm following up on a problem with my personal directory," Hu said. "Mr. Kaplewski had another matter to address across campus and I told him I would save him the trouble."

"Buddy," Margray said, immediately belligerent, "I've worked with Kaplewski for a while now and I know one thing about him beyond a doubt—he absolutely hates it when amateurs touch his system."

Hu just stared at him.

"Care to try again?" Margray bullied him.

Hu bolted.

He ran for all he was worth. Margray looked after him, frozen in surprise, and then shook his head like a bull shaking off a failed run at a matador. Pumping his short legs, he barreled off after the administrator.

Hu reached the parking lot outside the computer center at a dead run, finding his four-year-old Honda Accord. He fumbled with the key, managed to start the vehicle and tore away.

Margray, hot on his heels, almost slammed into the door of his ancient Chevy pickup. He ripped open the unlocked door, not knowing why Hu was running, determined to chase him down and find out what was going on. Margray lived with a deep and abiding suspicion of his fellow man, on principle, and Hu's behavior was nothing short of incriminating. Margray didn't know *what* the man had done, but he was damned if he'd let him get away with it.

He fought with the wheel as they entered denser traffic on the roads around the college, flying down Ithaca's too-narrow streets and dodging the endless construction that threatened to turn the college town—already a nightmare mess of one-way streets and illogical traffic patterns—into a permanent parking lot.

Margray reached under his seat, feeling for the Colt Gold Cup 1911 that he was not supposed to have on campus. He pulled it from its leather holster. Shoving the pistol awkwardly in his waistband, he saw his opening and took it, punching the accelerator. The truck shot forward, trembling like a racehorse. As Hu's car drifted wide around a corner and into the parking lot of a convenience store, Margray cut him off, following as the Honda swerved. He brought the Chevy to a tire-scorching halt, stomping on the brakes and dragging the truck sideways, trapping the Honda between it and the wall of the convenience store.

Margray threw open his door and started toward the Honda.

Hu opened his own door and leveled a Sig-Sauer P-230, snapping off rounds as fast as he could pull the trigger.

Acting on the lessons of his weekend shooting classes, Margray sidestepped, drew his .45 and brought it on target as his thumb wiped the safety down and off. Two bullets erupted from the barrel in quick succession, slapping into Hu and spraying the Honda with its owner's blood.

Hu dropped, the Sig-Sauer falling from his limp fingers.

Mark Margray, engineer, concerned citizen, faithful Republican, and holder of a New York State pistol permit, looked down at the first and only man he had ever shot—and wondered what the hell had happened.

HUANG YAO AND HIS MEN saw to the loading of the methamphetamine with the other chemicals stored at the safehouse. The sizable shipment had arrived by special courier, disguised as pool chemicals. The fact that the safehouse had a tiny yard with no room for a pool, above- or in-ground, had not fazed the driver in the least. Huang Yao shook his head at the oblivious way these Americans led their lives, questioning nothing, concerned only with the three feet of air directly before their faces.

As field leader for Chang's special operations forces, the responsibility placed on Huang was significant. He was to see to the disposition of the chemicals, component substances dangerous enough by themselves, but volatile when exposed to one another. Only in the right proportions would the chemicals combine with the methamphetamine to generate the deadly nerve gas, and that could only happen with the treatment of special machinery.

The basement of the safehouse was filled with an elaborate layout of devices to be used in combining, treating and distilling the chemicals. Once prepared, the solids would sublimate on exposure to the air. They would be kept in airtight canisters until the moment of their release. Already, Huang had seen to the storage of ten canisters, each the size of a small beer keg—and each disguised to look like one, for what better cover was there in an American college town—in the basement. He had scrupulously tested their function, for if there was any break in their seals, the nerve agent would immediately become airborne.

Huang had seen footage of tests on lab mice, dogs and monkeys. The results has been disturbing, but not nearly as sobering as the footage of political prisoners used to test the final formulations of the compound. The gas, which had no name, entered the bloodstream directly through the skin. The first signs of exposure were heart palpitations and convulsions, accompanied by sudden and severe sweating.

Some test subjects frothed at the mouth like rabid dogs, while others did not. All collapsed in short order, their muscles contracting, as they felt their hearts hammering in their chests. When the heart muscle finally burst from the overwork brought on by the gas, hemorrhaging from the mouth, nose, eyes and ears signaled the imminence of death. If by some miracle the subject did not die from heart trauma, brain damage invariably resulted.

Huang had no desire to die like that, nor did he wish, if he failed to expire, to live out his days as a crippled vegetable.

Huang was a powerful man, more than a match for the two loyalists Chang employed as bodyguards. He'd shaved his head completely bald and affected no facial hair. Throwing himself into a punishing workout routine each morning, he kept himself in prime physical shape, drafting his fellow special operations agents for impromptu sparring sessions and weapons practice with unloaded firearms and sheathed knives. He was loyal to the People's Republic of China, he was loyal to the People's Liberation Army, and he believed ardently in the mission of the special operations teams working against America from without and within. Huang lived for the day that China would take its rightful role as world superpower, relegating the United States to the status of failing, faltering and crumbling empire.

Huang had been given two teams to help him accomplish his work. The first team, four men working with him in the safehouse, was busy arranging and securing the chemicals, keeping the most volatile combinations as far apart from one another as was possible. The second team, another squad of four, occupied the van Huang had appropriated. The van was parked several blocks from the safehouse, its hidden weaponry ready to be deployed should a contingency plan be required.

Once all was ready, they would wait for Chang's confirmation. Then, with the information obtained from their agent within the college they would see to it the canisters were deployed. The students and the politicians would be dead—and a new era for the People's Republic would begin. The Americans would be too busy chasing their own tails to bark at the rest of the world.

Syracuse, New York

DOREEN BROWN CHECKED HER hair in a small pocket mirror as staffers bustled around her, preparing the teleprompter and the peripheral packages for the noon news report. A veteran television personality, Brown was accustomed to the controlled chaos. She was looking forward to getting her first interview over with.

The network was cross-promoting with the unctuous Bobby Tortillo, easily the most prolific advertiser in central New York. Tortillo owned the largest chain of car dealerships in the state. His budget for promotion was so large that giant pictures of his face with the Tortillo Motors logo had been wrapped around almost every city bus. Tortillo starred in all of his own ads, his six-foot-four frame gone slowly to pot since his days as a college football player, capering about in a ten-gallon hat. His trademark cowboy yell was used in all of those ads and was universally loathed by the viewing public—who never seemed to loathe it enough to stop buying cars from his incredibly successful business.

The producer, Randy Rickson, swept through the room. "We're live in five, people," he said. Rickson was a good producer, and it was obvious to Doreen that he wasn't pleased about the inclusion of Bobby Tortillo, either.

"Ready, baby!" Tortillo announced loudly and unnecessarily from his spot in front of the green screen where he stood with Bill Jones. Jones was the station meteorologist and the only person in the studio whose skin did not crawl in the presence of Bobby Tortillo.

Staffers took their stations as the minutes counted down. Doreen scanned the stories they would be covering, which included the usual filler, a shooting in the usually peaceful town of Ithaca, and the lead, an accident involving Roger Kohler.

Doreen faced the camera, waiting for her signal. Tortillo started quivering, working himself up for his segment. Zack Farnsworth, the sports reporter, rolled his eyes. Doreen ignored them all as the intro music played and Rickson signaled her.

·"Good afternoon," she said smoothly, offering a cheerful smile that was absolutely insincere. "I'm Doreen Brown, and this is News Station 8 at Noon." She paused and turned for the camera switch. On the in-studio monitors, her head and shoulders were offset to allow space for the on-screen graphics that would highlight each packaged newsbyte.

"Embattled developer Roger Kohler, recently released on bail on charges including conspiracy and drug trafficking, was found dead in his home today, the victim of an apparent fall down a flight of stairs in his condominium," she said, emphasizing a word in each sentence with the cadence of a practiced anchor. "The Medical Examiner's office describes it as a freak accident."

"If you believe that," someone said off camera, "you're a bigger fool than that imbecile in the hat."

Doreen looked to Farnsworth, then searched for the voice. *Nobody* broke in during the newscast. She spotted a big, bearded man in a Syracuse police uniform.

She looked for Rickson, wondering if this was an unscheduled live interview. It was highly irregular, if so.

The cop stepped forward, drawing his pistol. Doreen's eyes grew wide in shock. As she watched, the man pulled the trigger.

Zack Farnsworth was struck in the neck. Blood sprayed, speckling Doreen's face, as the sports anchor fell out of his chair and dropped to the floor.

"What the hell are you *doing?*" Bobby Tortillo demanded. The cop whipped the gun around and started blasting the sloppy car salesman, the reports punishing Doreen's ears. She screamed and held her hands to her head, shaking, sinking down in her chair behind the desk.

Bobby Tortillo lost his cowboy hat as he slumped to his knees, his chest a ruin of .40-caliber bullet holes. His blood soaked the front of the shirt and leaked down his legs, a crimson tide that his splayed fingers could not stop. He stared at the cop in shock, not understanding. As Doreen looked on in horror, Bobby Tortillo flopped forward and landed directly on his face, his nose breaking with a sickening crunch.

"Does anyone else want to join them?" Gary Rook demanded. Doreen recognized him then, placing him despite the incongruous uniform. Channel 8 had run a morning update report that she'd anchored herself, in which an old ID photo of Rook had been used.

"You're…you're in the hospital, in a coma," Brown stammered.

"I checked myself out," he told her, waving the gun, drawing a second pistol and covering everyone in the studio. "I want you to know that I'm absolutely serious," he told them. "Anyone who resists me in any way will be shot. Anyone who attempts to leave this building will be shot, and if I don't catch them, I'll shoot one person in here for every one of you who escapes. Now—" he paused, glaring at the nearest cameraman "—I want that camera on me. Do it! You there," he said, gesturing to Rickson, who was standing protectively in front of a female staffer. "Get into that control booth and make sure I'm coming through in living color."

"What do you want?" Rickson demanded, his voice steady despite the threat.

"I want to leave a message for someone," Rook told him, the pistol pointing at Rickson's head. "You're all going to help me, or everyone last one of you is going to die."

13

Ithaca, New York

From his SUV, Mack Bolan surveyed the neighborhood. The houses were relatively small and close together, Cape Cods with white picket fences and well-maintained lawns. The area looked, to all appearances, to be quite peaceful.

The Executioner did not like it, not one bit. The hit on the safehouse could easily spill over to adjacent structures, igniting a firestorm that could claim many innocent lives. They would have to be very careful to contain whatever they found inside.

He unclipped his secure comm set from his combat harness, placing it behind his left ear and affixing the throat mike. The scrambled headset connected him directly to Jack Grimaldi.

"Jack, comm check."

"I hear you, Sarge."

"Clear here, too. You ready?"

"Out of sight and out of mind. Say the word and I'll drop in."

"Good. Wait for my signal."

"Out."

Bolan checked his war bag on the seat next to him. The local authorities wouldn't like it, but he was finished with soft probes. From the war bag he removed a mini-Uzi and its spare magazine pouch, strapping the pouch to his left leg and checking the placement of his other gear. He unfolded the metal stock of the weapon and, bracing it against his shoulder, left the truck, stalking toward the house.

The area was clear of neighbors and spectators as he crossed the road and circled the house. The back door appeared to be unguarded, but it was likely alarmed or rigged in some way. Bolan removed the breaching charge from a pouch on his web belt, placed the sticky mount above the knob of the back door and armed the electronic detonator. Then he stepped to one side. The automatic countdown ended in a high-pitched whine. The shaped explosion shattered the door lock and blew it inward. Inside, a pair of shotgun-shell metal tube booby traps were triggered by the door's movement, sending double-aught buck into the floor and ceiling. Bolan kicked the shattered and pockmarked wooden door, immediately spraying the area within, emptying the mini-Uzi of its 9 mm load.

He was not disappointed. A man dropped at the other end of the room, which turned out to be a kitchen. The body crumpled half-in and half-out of the doorway leading out of the kitchen to the rest of the house. He was a large man, wearing a black long-sleeved T-shirt and black fatigue pants. On the floor in front of him where it had fallen was an AK-47. Bolan bent, examined the Kalashnikov. From the markings, it was a Chinese knockoff. There was no doubt that this was the place and that those inside were involved in *something* dirty.

Daylight filtered in through the kitchen windows, which had been spray-painted with white paint to prevent those passing by from looking inside. The Executioner quickly unloaded the Chinese AK, jacked out the chambered round, popped the receiver cover and removed the bolt. He tossed the now useless weapon aside, throwing the bolt in another direction.

Footsteps, coming from the basement, trundled up a flight of stairs that emptied into the next room. Bolan quickly reloaded his Uzi and cocked it. The basement door slammed to one side, the doorknob taking a chunk out of the plaster wall behind it, as another man emerged. His Kalashnikov had a set of rails mounted under the barrel, where a combat flashlight had been affixed. Bolan changed his aim slightly and stitched the man across the face, before the Chinese operative could acquire a target. He dropped the AK and fell backward, tumbling down the stairs in a broken tangle. As Bolan entered the living room, he stepped around the boxes and drums of chemicals that cluttered the area.

Bolan stopped at the basement stairway. He listened. There was no movement from the upper floor, no telltale creaking of floorboards above. If people were up there, they were not moving and were not the priority.

Bolan eased the basement door open and pointed the Uzi one-handed down the steps. He caught a flash of movement and threw himself back. From beneath the open steps watching him through the slats, another Chinese operative opened fire with a handgun, the bullets ripping up through the wood. Bolan twisted, shoved the Uzi through a gap between two steps, and pulled the trigger, hosing the man from above. The 124-grain slugs punctured the top of his head and his shoulders, knocking him over onto his stomach. He was still.

The Executioner hustled double-time down the steps, the Uzi angling with him as he crouched to get sight of the basement.

Across the room, a single man stood amid the complicated machinery, distillation tubing and bubbling tanks of chemicals. The stink down there was terrible and made Bolan's eyes water. He knew there was a dangerous mix of toxins, many of them explosion hazards. Combined, they could erupt in a fireball that would level the house and probably many around it. Bolan lowered his weapon.

"I am Huang," the Chinese operative told him.

"Justice Department," Bolan said. "Put your hands behind your head and get down on your knees."

"I cannot let you leave here alive," Huang said, approaching. He had to climb around several stainless-steel drums and avoid a table laden with mysterious-looking devices.

"Stop right there," Bolan said, raising the Uzi.

"You are wise to hesitate," Huang said, still approaching. "The chemicals you see here, in varying states of preparation, are not the biggest threat." He pointed to the ten drums stacked against one wall. "The slightest loss of integrity in those canisters will release a deadly nerve gas. It does not burn. If this building explodes, the explosion will do more than level the house above us. It will release the gas, killing all who breathe for a square block, perhaps two."

Bolan lowered the Uzi—he couldn't chance it. "I'm giving you a chance to surrender," he said.

"That is generous of you." Huang began pushing up the sleeves of his black commando sweater, worn over black fatigue pants. His feet, shod in combat boots, scuffed the concrete floor. "As I said, I cannot let you leave here alive."

Huang struck without warning. He fired a straight punch that Bolan just managed to slip, the blow glancing off the Executioner's temple hard enough to make him see stars. He front-kicked automatically, catching Huang solidly in the shin. The big Chinese operative grunted and stepped back, his hands raised.

Bolan backed off a few paces, setting his Uzi carefully on the floor. Then he drew his fighting knife. The razor-sharp combat dagger slid easily from its sheath.

"We can do it that way," Huang said. He drew a Kalashnikov bayonet from his belt, the bowie-shaped blade honed to an edge rivaling Bolan's. Blade held before him, his off arm held in front of his body with the blade low, Huang advanced.

Bolan reversed his knife and stepped aside as Huang slashed. He moved off at an angle, letting Huang's slash pass him, then entered and slashed at the knife arm, checking and controlling as he did so. Huang howled and struck with the butt of his knife on the backhand, but Bolan ducked aside again. Huang stepped out of range; Bolan stayed where he was, waiting, the knife ready.

Huang was strong, but not terribly fast. It was clear he'd had some training with the knife, but Bolan had the advantage of vastly greater experience. As Huang struck again, Bolan scissored his knife arm, bringing his own blade across the top of his adversary's arm while slapping the arm through that blade with his off hand. Blood sprayed and Huang's knife fell from suddenly numb fingers.

Bolan brought his knife around in a backhand, directly into Huang's throat. He had no other choice— the Chinese operative was big and strong enough that the Executioner could not afford to trade blows with him, could not chance losing the fight and losing control of the cache of toxins. The tip of the knife was buried in Huang's neck. Bolan ripped it free as he stepped through, bringing his off hand in a guard before his body. Huang gurgled an anguished cry as he collapsed, clutching at his throat, his blood pouring from the gaping tear.

Bolan took a step back and watched Huang, waiting to see if another strike would be necessary. He watched as Huang bled out, his eyes turning glassy as he stared at the ceiling.

After wiping his knife clean on Huang's pants, Bolan sheathed it and retrieved his Uzi. He swept the rest of the house room by room, verifying that it was empty.

As he made his way from one bedroom to a second upstairs, he heard someone speaking softly in Chinese.

Stepping back, Bolan brought the Uzi up and fired a burst into the closed closet door. When he was satisfied, he ripped open the door. Another Chinese operative rolled out, dead at his feet, still clutching a wireless phone.

"Jack," Bolan said into the comm set, "heads up. Sweep the area."

JACK GRIMALDI BROUGHT THE Cobra gunship lower, buzzing the Ithaca neighborhood and causing passersby to gape. People left their homes to watch him. He was not concerned with them, though he knew he and Bolan would have plenty of explaining to do if the local cops got their hands on the pair before Brognola got to them. The Cobra's rotors pummeled the air and the gunship swept over the street. Satisfied, Grimaldi gained altitude and swept in larger circles.

Then he saw the van.

It looked like a conversion van, with tinted windows and thick, aftermarket wheels. Painted silver, with a large metal crash bar over the grille, it could have been any of hundreds of such rides to be found in New York. It rode very low to the ground, however, as if loaded to the limits of its shocks. It was also burning rubber for all the engine was worth, laying down a trail of smoke as it barreled down the street three blocks from the Chinese safehouse.

"Sarge," Grimaldi said into his comm set, "I think I have what you're looking for."

"One of them made a cell phone call," Bolan informed him.

"Probably the 'go' signal, then," Grimaldi explained. "I've got a heavy van fleeing the scene. It looks suspicious."

"Can you get in front of them?" Bolan asked him.

"It's too tight, Sarge," Grimaldi said apologetically. "I can fire the cannon or my rocket pods from the rig here in my seat, but that's going to get messy fast in a real residential sort of way."

"Tail them," Bolan told him. "I'm in the truck now and headed your way."

"West, five blocks," Grimaldi told him. "I'll course correct you as we go."

WITHIN THE VAN, HUANG'S contingency squad prepared their personal weapons as they strapped themselves into their seats with five-point harnesses. They took their operating stations. The driver pressed an arming switch on the console between the front seats.

From the sides of the van, two rocket pods extended from flush-fit panels in the flanks of the vehicle. These were connected to targeting and fire control terminals built into the rear chairs of the van. From the passenger's seat, the third gunner activated the closed-circuit targeting camera connected to the unit on the roof. When he did so, a dual machine gun mount rotated into position.

"Yes?" the voice on the other end of the phone answered.

"Comrade Chang, we have a problem," the operative informed him. "The safehouse has been hit and all within have been lost. We have lost control of the equipment and the supplies."

Chang was silent for a moment. "How—" he started to ask, then thought better of it. "What of Huang?"

"We believe he is dead or captured," the operative said. "The report from the safehouse was cut short as Tang Lu tried to make it. I heard shots. I believe him to be dead. The Americans have found us out."

"The operation is completely compromised," Chang said. It was not a question.

"Yes, General."

Chang was silent for a long moment. "Very well," he said at last. "Execute Omega Option. You understand?"

"Yes, General."

"You must not be taken alive. You understand this as well, yes?"

"I do, General."

"Then do your work. Make them pay. If we cannot carry out the plan, we can at least shake America's faith in its invulnerability."

"Yes, General." The driver closed the connection and dropped the wireless phone on the floor of the vehicle. "Fire at will," he informed his squad.

GRIMALDI WATCHED IN horror from his vantage point as a plume of smoke erupted from the vehicle. The rocket slammed into a church, blowing a gaping crater in the stone structure. Another rocket fired from the opposite side of the van, connecting with a parked SUV and blowing the truck into the air in a cloud of flame and broken glass. The truck landed back on its flattened tires, its axles broken or bent, its failing car alarm bleating impotently.

"Sarge!" he said over the comm set. "They're firing heavy ordnance into civilians!"

"Take them, Jack!" Bolan ordered over the link. "I'm a block away. Take them and I'll mop up!"

Grimaldi did not hesitate. As risky as what he was about to do could be in a residential neighborhood, it was less dangerous than allowing the murderous occupants of the van to continue their rampage. He armed his electric 20 mm cannon and fired, strafing the roof of the van. The vehicle shuddered but did not stop. The roof was apparently armor plated, that armor keeping enough rounds out of the interior to shield the occupants and allow the van to stay mobile. Grimaldi did allow himself grim satisfaction at the destruction of the machine gun mount on the roof, however.

As the van rolled on, two more rockets flew from its sides. The small but deadly devices carried as much punch as an RPG—and more, despite their compact design. One destroyed the porch of a house. Another flew into the windshield of a moving Toyota, burst through the rear window and traveled on until it lost enough altitude to impact the pavement. The rocket blew a gigantic pothole in the street, spraying asphalt shrapnel into vehicles and into people running from the carnage.

"Jesus, Sarge!" Grimaldi said. "I have to use something heavier."

"Do it, Jack!"

Grimaldi, his fingers steady on the stick, dropped the chopper as low as he possibly could. He lined up the targeting reticule and pushed the button.

The missile pushed itself free of the launch tube. Its rocket motor ignited, carrying the antitank weapon on a line of smoke and fire to the Chinese death van.

The explosion sent the van flipping over and over laterally, ripping up a section of the street and taking out several parked cars. Civilians screamed. Grimaldi was thankful that he could see no one directly hit by his missile or the rolling van. He brought the chopper up, breaking his line of sight to the target, rotating to scan for other possible threats.

"They're down, Striker," Grimaldi reported. He glanced at the war-torn city street. "Jesus, Sarge, we're going to be in deep shit."

BOLAN BROUGHT HIS SUV TO a stop several yards from the smoking, crumpled attack van. He threw open his door and almost ran for the van, drawing his .44 Magnum Desert Eagle. Face tight with anger as he saw how much damage had been done to the innocent civilians of Ithaca, he advanced on the wrecked vehicle and adopted a two-hand firing grip.

The van lay on its driver's side, the rocket pod still visible on the passenger side smoking idly as the dead engine ticked and gasoline leaked from somewhere near the rear of the vehicle. Bolan made eye contact with the driver, still harnessed in his seat. The Chinese operative pointed his weapon at Bolan.

The Executioner fired three times, the .44 slugs tearing into the driver's head and chest, erasing forever the hostile expression on his face.

One of the rear doors of the van opened on squealing, bent hinges. Bolan used the death van for cover as two Chinese operatives, one with a Kalashnikov, one with a Makarov pistol, opened fire from either side. Bolan dived left, catching the Makarov gunner. The .44 hollowpoint round from the Desert Eagle tore through his arm lengthwise, shattering bone and digging a furrow through the flesh. The operative shrieked and stumbled, clawing at his ruined arm.

As he stepped away and around the van to the left, Bolan kept the vehicle between himself and the Kalashnikov gunner. Several bullets burned past him, high and wide, as the gunman shot blindly in Bolan's direction.

Too late Bolan recognized the ruse. The gunner at the van had kept the soldier occupied. When the shooting stopped, Bolan heard a woman scream.

"Do not fire, or you hit this woman!" one of the two Chinese agents shouted in thickly accented English.

Bolan let his Desert Eagle fall to low ready even as he dropped the magazine and slammed a fresh one home. "Don't do it!" he cautioned.

The two enemy operative moved from behind the van. The Kalashnikov gunner kept his weapon aimed at Bolan. The second man had his arm around the throat of a middle-aged woman wearing hospital scrubs. The woman was terrified; Bolan could see it in her eyes. Her captor had the blade of an AK bayonet at her throat. Around them, buildings burned, people screamed or watched while hiding behind cars and buildings, and sirens could be heard in the distance. The Ithaca police were coming. Overhead, the drumbeat of Grimaldi's chopper was the like the beating of a desperate heart.

"Jack, have you got a shot?" Bolan subvocalized.

"I can take the one with the rifle," Grimaldi said, "but it will be tricky. They're awfully close together."

"Understood."

To the Chinese agent, he said, "You're not walking out of here."

"No," the agent holding the woman said, "we're not. But we will not die at your hand!"

The one with the rifle turned to look at his comrade. He said something quickly in Chinese. The hostage-taker said something back angrily.

"Jack," Bolan said, "do it now."

The world exploded as 20 mm projectiles shredded the man with the AK. The sidewalk beneath him was churned under the heavy bombardment, raising a cloud of concrete dust and pelting the other operative and his hostage with stone shrapnel. The woman screamed again, but it was the break Bolan needed. When her captor clutched at his face to clear his eyes of debris, the knife wavered.

Bolan raised the Desert Eagle and launched a single .44 round into the man's eye, snapping his head back. He fell, the knife still clutched in his hand. The woman, sobbing uncontrollably, simply ran. Bolan noted her direction; she was heading for the police cars that were even now surrounding them.

He stood, the Desert Eagle smoking in his fist, the Chinese van and countless cars and buildings smoking all around him. They had stopped the Chinese, but at a heavy cost.

His work was not done.

14

Hours after the hit on the safehouse, Bolan was still in Ithaca, Grimaldi backing him up. He had contacted the Farm after the disastrous terrorist rampage through Ithaca, only to be informed that Gary Rook was alive, well, and taking hostages in Syracuse. The Farm could not offer much backup. Able Team and Phoenix Force were deployed in equally critical trouble zones. There had, however, been time to mobilize a squad of black-suits, Stony Man Farm-trained commandos, who had taken charge of the situation—after some bullying thanks to Brognola's Justice Department authority. The locals were screaming to high heaven about that, but it wouldn't make a lot of difference in the long run.

Rook had taken no more lives since first seizing the station, which was the only reason the blacksuits and those authorities on site were trying to wait him out. The Stony Man team would be content to wait for Bolan's intervention and guidance before breaching the build-ing—unless Rook killed someone else or indicated that he was about to do so.

Syracuse was a city in shock. Torn by violence out of all proportion to its usual woes, the city now endured televised murders and the ranting of a dangerously unstable man who still held the lives of dozens of others in his hands. Rook had been broadcasting for hours, holding several staff members at gunpoint on camera the entire time. He had made a long, rambling plea that was an exhortation to avoid drugs. He'd spent time condemning himself for the things he'd done and then started enumerating a list of crimes against him by "the establishment" and local law enforcement. Several times he spoke of a commando, whose presence he demanded. He did not seem capable of maintaining his line of thought, and he appeared to be deteriorating rapidly. Whatever injuries he had suffered were taking their toll.

The situation in Ithaca had gone from bad to worse, however, and there was no way Bolan could return to Syracuse until it was resolved.

Cao Chang, with nothing to lose and with his plans blown wide open, had ordered his people to seize the office building where he rented space. Bolan had a nasty feeling of déjà vu when the first reports were brought to him. This, time, however, thanks to plenty of phone jockeying from Brognola, he had the cooperation of local law enforcement. A complete SWAT team was rolling with Bolan and Grimaldi to take the office building.

Bolan, Grimaldi and the SWAT team gathered one block from the building.

"Listen up," Bolan said, taking charge. The SWAT commander, Meyers, stepped forward, his flared helmet under his arm.

"My team will work with you, Mr. Cooper," Meyers informed him, "but I want to say for the record that I don't agree with the games your superiors are playing with jurisdiction."

Bolan didn't recognize any superiors, but he did not argue with the man. Meyers stood a head shorter than his fellow SWAT troopers but carried himself with an energy and a presence that commanded respect. Wearing wire-rimmed glasses strapped behind his bald head, under his safety goggles, he looked over Bolan—who was preparing his mini-Uzi and had his Beretta 93-R and Desert Eagle in their respective holsters—and Grimaldi in turn. The pilot carried his shotgun and looked a little out of place next to the blacksuited Bolan and the SWAT troops in their BDUs, but he also looked as confident as any of them.

"They've got the first floor completely blocked off," Meyers reported. "There are a lot of them in there, too, but we've got no firm numbers. They're heavily armed. My spotters saw AK-47s and a news vehicle took automatic fire before we forced the reporters back behind the barricade. There's been no indication of heavier weapons."

"Don't count on that," Bolan warned. "They could have RPGs and other ordnance."

Meyers nodded. "Let's move," he said. Bolan nodded back and the group approached the building.

SEALED WITHIN HIS OFFICE, Chang sat behind his desk with his bodyguards standing at attention on either side. In the outer office and the corridor beyond, he could hear his men bustling about, preparing defenses, digging in and checking weapons.

It had happened so quickly that he did not know if he could grasp it. In hours, in *minutes,* months of planning, years of work, had been swept away. Chang and his people had stood up to the great enemy of the West, the arrogant, violent, greedy bully that was the United States of America, expecting little resistance from the fat, ignorant, lazy American people. They had worked knowing that they had behind them the full might of the People's Republic of China, the power of the People's Liberation Army. What had gone so wrong?

It should have been easy. Instead, Chang and his people had repeatedly come face-to-face with an implacable, determined foe who struck them down before they could destroy what the Americans had built, what the Americans had stolen, what the Americans simply *had.*

He had thought to hit the enemy where he thought the enemy weakest, most unsuspecting, most unprepared. But he had discovered a foe more willing to meet him on the field of battle than he had ever imagined.

Chang had changed into the informal black BDU uniform and combat boots that his operatives favored when not undercover among the Americans. Before him, on his desk, lay a submachine gun with a folding stock, a laser and a flashlight attached. Many of these weapons were in the hands of his men, who also had a small supply of RPGs—useless in the close confines of the building—and quite a few Chinese-manufactured Kalashnikov clones.

Filling a messenger bag with loaded magazines for the submachine gun, he then loaded the weapon and cocked the bolt. Reports were coming in over the two-way radios everyone carried. The American law-enforcement officers, as well as an American Chang suspected was the architect of his many violent defeats, were outside the barricaded building. It was inevitable that they would attempt entry. They would succeed. Chang and his people could not hold out indefinitely.

Chang did not have to do so.

His men would fight loyally, believing themselves to be laying down their lives for the greater good of the People's Republic. He had filled their heads with notions of heroes' funerals, their families being granted privileges and luxuries, their names remembered in song and official records. He knew it would guarantee their enthusiasm, their ferocity. While his men fought, he would make his way to the lowest level of the building and into the painstakingly built escape tunnel. Dug by workers whom Chang had personally executed, the tunnel was known only to him. It would take him to the underground parking lot of an adjoining building, where Chang kept a car—registered to another nonexistent American, an identity he had appropriated through Song's contacts years previously—fueled and ready to go. He would escape when the furor died down and no one would be the wiser. What's more, he would be assumed dead. Chang patted a cargo pocket of his pants to make sure he had everything he required.

In reality, his men would not be feted as heroes of the State. They would be disavowed—perhaps even erased, made unpersons, to grant China plausible deniability. There were enough links to the People's Republic among the dead bodies of Huang's operatives. While they had been very careful, he would not be surprised if there was incriminating evidence to be found at the safehouse. In any event the plan was a total failure, the nerve agent components recovered by the Americans, the plan exposed—though, to whom, Chang was not entirely sure—and even poor, foolish Zhongchao Hu eliminated, gunned down so ironically by one of the gun-toting rednecks who peopled this blighted land. There was something obscene, yet terribly fitting about the sleeper agent's demise. The news had only recently reached him in this now-besieged refuge.

Chang briefly considered composing a final message, or a will of sorts, to leave for posterity. He had no family, no associates with whom he was close. Still, he thought it would be unfortunate if he died and left nothing behind. Then he caught himself and shook off his anxiety. There was no good to come of it—he had to focus on the task of escaping in the confusion. Chiding himself for his negativity, Chang dismissed all such notions, hefted his weapon and tested the laser and flashlight units. It would be time soon.

He heard the first explosion, then, muffled by the floors between him and the ground level. A breaching charge, most likely. The Americans would be on their way.

Chang's men would be there to greet them.

MEYERS AND ANOTHER officer, Goodline, adopted a two-by-two formation with troopers Tanenbaum and Mac-

Gregor. Covering each other in pairs, the men led the way as Bolan, Grimaldi and the rest of the SWAT team followed. They breached the door, and Meyers and Goodline were first through the opening.

The took heavy fire as soon as they were past the entrance. Bolan recognized the hollow metallic rattle of AKs, as well as the stuttering of machine pistols. The Chinese operatives were well armed and there were many of them. To fight their way up level by level using only small arms would be bloody and slow.

The Chinese forces occupied positions above the lobby level of the building. The elevators had been wedged open with screwdrivers and other hand tools, but no one in his right mind would attempt to use them anyway. They were death traps. The SWAT team advanced on the stairwell, taking more fire but driving the closest gunman back as they answered with a barrage of 9 mm and 5.56 mm rounds.

"Masks, masks, masks!" Goodline called back to troopers, on a signal from Meyers. All of the SWAT cops donned gas masks. Bolan and Grimaldi did likewise, using borrowed units. A trooper in the rear hurried up, carrying a heavy multichamber tear gas grenade launcher.

Meyers tapped the man twice, deliberately, on the shoulder. The masked SWAT trooper nodded, aimed the launcher and began pumping CS gas grenades up the stairwells, bouncing them off walls to get them around corners. The grenades began spewing gas and the troopers could hear their enemies coughing and choking.

"Now!" Meyers ordered. Two troopers took backup positions in the lobby, securing the rear. The remainder, including Bolan and Grimaldi, began scrambling up the stairs.

In the haze of CS gas they could feel the gunmen before and sometimes to either side of them as they moved. Meyers and his men quickly began engaging targets. Bolan and Grimaldi did the same, Bolan's Uzi burning out short bursts and Grimaldi's shotgun dealing close-range devastation as the SWAT team fired their own AR-15s and MP-5s. Bolan dropped a coughing combatant at the top of the stairwell, punching holes through the man's pelvis and abdomen. Grimaldi administered a mercy blast from his 12-gauge as he came up following the Executioner. Another man fell when Goodline shot him twice in the chest and once in the head with his AR-15. Still others were dropped or driven back as they struggled to function in the CS mist, their eyes burning, their throats closing.

At the first floor the troopers started going room to room, using their weapon-mounted lights when necessary to peer into dark corners or pierce the worst of the gas they had distributed. Goodline and Meyers took one doorway, sweeping the room with short bursts, dropping a pair of Chinese who were preparing to load an RPG to fire at the SWAT barricades from the window. Tanenbaum and MacGregor took one room high and low, and shot two more Chinese agents center of mass while dodging 7.62 mm fire.

It was slow going. Bolan and Grimaldi took a room of their own. The Executioner kicked in the door. Inside, behind an overturned desk, a single gunman armed with a .45-caliber handgun punched 230-grain rounds over Grimaldi's head. Bolan twisted, turning sideways, bringing up the Uzi one-handed and firing as he went. The rounds climbed up the agent's body, ripping him open from groin to neck.

"This is taking too long, Sarge," Grimaldi complained. They repeated the drill on the next floor, and then the third—CS gas first, then clearing from room to room. More operatives were found and all were killed. Officer Tanenbaum took a round through the leg and was helped clear by another of the troopers, but the team remained unscathed otherwise. Bolan ran out of loaded magazines for his Uzi, so he hid the weapon in a trash can on the third floor and switched to his Beretta 93-R. They fought their way to Chang's office on the upper floors.

They continued with their grim, bloody task, the operation reminding Bolan of the urban warfare he'd waged in every corner of the globe. It was never easy. It was never preferable. It was, all too often, necessary.

In the confusion, no one saw the single, diminutive Chinese man making his way back down the stairs directly behind Officers Tanenbaum and Piccoroli.

"I've got you," Piccoroli told the wounded Tanenbaum.

Tanenbaum heard the noise behind them. He turned—

Chang fired a burst from his weapon, dumping half the magazine into Tanenbaum's chest. The wounded man fell over himself and down the steps to the next landing, blood and bone spraying.

Piccoroli acted on instinct, grabbing the hot barrel of the submachine gun and shoving it away from his body. He yanked, pulling Chang off balance as the agent tried to retain his weapon. Piccoroli drove a knee into Chang's abdomen and then dropped a vicious elbow on the back of his neck, stripping the gun from Chang's grasp. The Chinese man went down hard, gasping, stars floating in his vision.

"You son of a bitch," Piccoroli roared. "That man had a family!" He leveled the weapon and Chang's eyes widened. The American storm trooper meant to finish him with his own weapon, and in cold blood.

A single gunshot rang out, louder than the sounds of furious combat filtering down from the levels of above. Chang opened his eyes to find the American policeman on the floor, an entry wound in the back of his head and a ragged exit wound obscuring his face.

From the landing above, one of Chang's burly bodyguards descended, blood of his own smeared on one side of his face and an AKM assault rifle clutched in his hands.

"Yang Te is dead, sir," the bodyguard said. It occurred to Chang that he had not known the other man's name, nor did he know *this* man's name. They had been with him, silent and reassuring, for so long that he had forgotten.

"How did you escape?" Chang asked, retrieving his gun.

"I crept away as you did, in the confusion."

"That is good," Chang lied. "Come with me. We must reach the basement level."

When they neared the ground floor they slowed their pace, taking the steps quietly. Then the bodyguard leaped the last steps and opened fire, catching one trooper completely flat-footed and dodging return fire from the other. Chang got off a burst that took the other American in the belly. He waited patiently while his bodyguard stood over the wounded American and shot him in the head.

When they reached the basement level without further incident, Chang motioned for the bodyguard to follow as he located the hidden entrance to the escape tunnel. He first removed a metal grate on what appeared to be a ventilation duct. Within, he pulled a lever, which activated hydraulics connected to the passageway door. The door slid quietly open from a section of the wall, where it looked like unbroken cinder block before the concealing mortar cracked and the door pulled free. Chang entered and his man obediently followed.

THERE WERE THREE operatives holed up in Chang's office. They had the room booby-trapped with an explosive improvised from an RPG. Officer MacGregor, an older member of the force who had seen a lot in his time with SWAT, noticed the trip wire and warned everyone off. He carefully removed the trip wire and pin, kicking the RPG shell into Chang's office for good measure.

The agents inside Chang's office had opened fire. Bolan and Grimaldi waited for a lull in the firing as the Chinese changed magazines, then took the room from either side, high and low.

"Clear," Bolan announced, his voice muffled in his gas mask.

"Clear," Meyers said from the doorway.

The call was echoed by the other troopers in the outer office and beyond.

Bolan surveyed the office, now strewed with shells, reeking of tear gas and splashed with gore.

Stony Man Farm had transmitted pictures to Bolan's

secure phone. The Executioner had studied them thoroughly. He frowned, planning his next step.

Nowhere among the bodies was Cao Chang.

Syracuse, New York

DOREEN BROWN HAD NEVER known such terror. Gary Rook had secured everyone in the broadcast booth, using phone cords and lengths of coaxial cable to bind their hands and feet. He had made them kneel on the floor along one wall, by the green screen. For the rest of the day and through the night, well into the morning, he had harangued them, avoiding all attempts from outside to establish a dialogue with him. Eventually he had allowed his prisoners to use the restrooms one and two at a time, threatening to execute everyone else in the room if his prisoners did not hobble back to him when they were finished.

Doreen had never seen so much blood. She had never before felt so helpless, at another human being's mercy so totally. She was exhausted and in pain and completely at a loss. Would it never end? She felt as if she might lose her mind.

For his part, Gary Rook was clearly insane and failing quickly. He was getting worse with each passing hour. For some time he had contented himself with ranting into the cameras, speaking of his deceased daughter. His paranoia had grown stronger the longer he spoke. For at least an hour he had railed against the "commando" who had tried to kill him, who had denied him justice, who didn't understand...most of the rest hadn't made much sense.

All the while, Rook, still wearing the police uniform,

had waved around one, sometimes two pistols, occasionally stopping to point them at some of his hostages. He'd done it to Doreen twice. The muzzle of the pistol looked impossibly large as she stared it down, and she imagined she could see the copper head of the bullet waiting at the end of the barrel, waiting to explode and take away from her everything she had ever known. The second time Rook had pointed that pistol at her, she had passed out, sprawling between the corpses on the floor. When she awoke, her fingers were sticky with Bobby Tortillo's blood.

Rook had lost steam in the past hour. He had spent most of it simply staring at the camera, his demeanor one of a man who was exhausted but still very hostile. He leaned on a stool taken from the control booth and sat before Camera 1, insisting that the station continue broadcasting. He watched himself on the in-studio monitor, looking for something only he understood. Doreen found herself praying to God to get her through this. *Please*, she implored, *let me leave here and see my husband and children again.*

THE POLICE OFFICERS AND blacksuits manning the barricades moved one of the barriers so Bolan's SUV could pass. Bolan, with Grimaldi in the passenger seat, guided the vehicle as close to the Channel 8 building as he dared.

The soldier was not happy about leaving things unfinished with Chang, but he was also smart enough to know that there would be other opportunities. Justice found everyone, sooner or later. That was the nature of his War Everlasting.

"You sure about this, Sarge?" Grimaldi asked.

"A lot of people are dead, Jack," he told the Stony Man pilot. "I refuse to let Gary Rook take any more innocent lives."

"The locals could handle this."

"They could," Bolan admitted. "But how many people will they lose in the meantime? Rook's unstable, perhaps completely unhinged. He's hurting, and he doesn't care who gets in his way. He'll chew up as many people as he can before they take him down, probably kill all the hostages and a fair number of law-enforcement officers. I can prevent all that."

"You can try, you mean," Grimaldi said.

"There are no guarantees," Bolan said. "There never have been and there never will be. It's been a lot of years, Jack. Do you really think I won't go?"

"Of course not," Grimaldi said, grinning. "But someone has to look out for you."

"Keep an eye on things out here," Bolan said.

He left the truck and walked to the inner barricades, where the blacksuit in charge greeted him. "Treble," the man said with just a hint of a New York City accent. "You'd be Cooper?" Bolan nodded. "They said you were comin' down," Treble acknowledged.

"You going in there?" Treble asked dubiously.

"I don't have a choice," Bolan said. "The same rules of engagement apply. If he kills me, or if he starts targeting hostages, your team is a go. Take him out and prevent further loss of life. As long as he stays focused on me, however—" Bolan looked Treble in the eye, making sure there was no doubt as to his orders "—you leave him to me. He's *mine*."

"Understood," Treble said.

15

Syracuse, New York

"Gary Rook!"

Rook roused from his lethargy, trying hard to focus. Had he heard his name?

The door to the studio opened slowly. Rook's head whipped up and he brought one of the Smith & Wesson pistols on target.

Bolan stepped through the door.

"Well," Rook said, fully focused, his eyes blazing. He stood and moved closer, his gun aimed at the Executioner's chest. "As I live and breathe," he said. "The man in black, come to collect me."

"My name is Cooper," Bolan said. "I'm with the Justice Department."

"That's a tired old song," Rook said, shaking his head. The barrel of the Smith & Wesson never wavered.

"You don't need to do this, Gary," the Executioner told him. "These people have done you no harm. You've told everyone. How many hours have you been on the air, Gary? Don't you think you've told the world what you wanted to tell them?"

"You don't understand," Rook told him.

"But I do. I understand better than anyone."

"Shut up!" Rook gestured with the pistol. "Put your weapons down! Two fingers on the trigger guard, put them on the floor! Now!"

Bolan steeled himself. This was when the situation would become delicate. Confronting Rook alone was having the desired effect, focusing all of the psychotic ex-Marine's attention on one man. Bolan knew Rook blamed him for denying him the bloody revenge he'd sought for so long. But Bolan's only real concern was for the hostages. He had to get Rook away from them, get the innocents out of the line of fire. Nearby, in front of the studio's green screen, several men and women cowered amid coagulated pools of blood from the two corpses Rook had left in his wake. If Bolan couldn't hold Rook's focus, the blacksuit-led force of cops and SWAT troops would have no choice but to the storm the building. There was no telling how many people might die in the ensuing carnage. It was an unacceptable risk.

"Weapons down!" Rook repeated. He raised his arm at full extension, the Smith & Wesson pointing at Bolan's face.

"I'm not going to do that," Bolan informed him. He kept his hands up, palms out, away from his body. Rook could shoot him at any time, but the Executioner was counting on the man wanting more than to simply drop Bolan where he stood.

Rook's expression hardened. "Do it or I'll kill you."

"You might," Bolan said, "but I don't think you'll do it like this."

"You're gambling with your life, soldier," Rook said.

"I've gambled with my life for more years than you know," Bolan told him, taking a step closer, his hands still held before his body in a gesture of surrender. "Tell me something. What would your daughter think of what you've done?"

"Everything I did, I did for Jennifer. To help her rest in peace. To help me rest in peace. To take back a little of what they took from us. They robbed me of everything. They took my life. They took the only person who was left, the only person who cared. Are you going to tell me those drug-running gangbangers didn't have it *coming?*"

"Maybe they did," Bolan told him. "What about that baby?"

"What?"

"The baby. You remember," Bolan prodded him, "from the meth house you hit, the trailer that blew up."

"I don't know what you're talking about."

"Sure you do," Bolan said. "You remember. There was a man and a woman. There was a crib in the room. You shot them both. You didn't care if you hit the crib or not. There was a baby in there."

Rook stared at him.

"What about those people?" Bolan asked, jerking his chin toward the two dead men on the floor, a near-hysterical woman kneeling between the corpses. "What did they do to you? What did they do to Jennifer? How are they involved?"

Rook looked at the bodies as if it was the first time he'd ever seen them. "I…I don't…"

"Listen to me, Rook," Bolan told him. "These are innocent people. They're not part of your war. Leave them out of it."

Rook looked back to Bolan. His arm, and the pistol held in his hand, dropped a few inches. "How can I...I don't know...I..."

"Let's step outside," Bolan told him. "Into the hallway."

Rook gestured with his pistol, waving in the direction of the door. "Go, then. We'll go."

Bolan backed out, keeping his eyes on Rook, maintaining the fragile connection between them.

Rook followed him into the long corridor. At the far end of the hall were elevators and a stairwell. At the end nearest Bolan was a door leading to a small secondary foyer—and then outside. Through the window in that door, Rook would be able to see beyond the plate-glass foyer to the array of police, blacksuits, SWAT troops, reporters, and spectators behind, the operators close to a series of barricades, the spectators corralled beyond that.

"Do you see?" Bolan asked the unstable Rook. "You've had your audience. You've made your statement. They've all heard it. The CNY Purists are smashed. Their leader is gone. The man who hired them is dead. Any larger connections have been handled by my people and those above them."

"What are you saying?" Rook asked.

"It's over, Gary," Bolan told him. "Put down your guns. Give yourself up."

Rook looked, for a heartbeat, as if he was considering it. Then his head snapped up and his eyes narrowed.

"Oh, you're not bad," he said, all the confusion and weakness gone from his voice. In place of the broken, mentally unstable man Bolan had first seen was the vigilante, the cunning operator and combat veteran who had killed so many and managed to elude Bolan and the cops repeatedly.

"Don't go for your gun," Rook told him. "Not yet. Back up. Back up all the way." He swung his pistol in the direction of the studio doors, which had small panes of glass in them. "Do it or I'll empty this into that room and we'll see who I hit before you take me."

Bolan nodded once. He backed up until he was roughly a foot from the door to the foyer. Rook did the same, until he was near the stairwell access door.

Calmly, his eyes on Bolan the whole time, Rook holstered his weapon. He left the thumb-break open.

"Reach around with two fingers of your left hand," Rook told Bolan. "Unsnap the holster on that hogleg you're packing."

Bolan complied, slipping the thumb-break on his tactical thigh holster, freeing the .44 Magnum Desert Eagle for a fast draw. He took a breath, relaxed. He watched as Rook did the same, shaking out his right hand. Bolan wiped his right palm against his abdomen, slowly, wiping it free of any sweat or grit that might have accumulated there.

"I wish you understood," Rook told him. "I wish you could see what I fight for."

"I know what you think you're fighting for," Bolan told him. "It's not—"

Rook's hand went for his gun as Bolan spoke. The

Executioner had expected the trick. His own hand shot for the Desert Eagle, mashing the web of his hand high and tight on the grip, his fingers clenching around the grip as his index finger paused above the trigger. The big weapon cleared the holster, the Desert Eagle coming up into a two-hand hold as his support hand found the weapon in front of his chest.

The gunshots—Rook's smaller .40-caliber round and the thunderclap from Bolan's .44 Magnum round— rang out almost at the same time.

Gary Rook was on the floor.

Bolan looked behind him, saw the bullet hole in the glass of the door's window and the spiderweb cracks in the plate glass foyer beyond. The holes followed a straight line from Rook's pistol to the spot where Bolan had been standing before he stepped to the side.

The soldier went to where Rook had fallen, still covering him with the Desert Eagle.

Rook's eyes opened.

He scissored his legs, catching Bolan and dropping him to his knees. Rook punched Bolan's arm on the inside of his forearm with all his strength. Bolan's fingers went numb and he dropped the big pistol. He pistoned a palm strike into Rook's face, snapping the vigilante's head back, then surged forward.

Rook twisted, rolling over, trying to get Bolan beneath him. The Executioner shrimped his way out of the attempted hold and kicked Rook in the ankle, his leg firing parallel to the floor as he supported his torso on his forearms. Something in Rook's ankle snapped and he screamed. Instead of falling, he hopped to one side.

Bolan leaped to his feet. The feeling was returning to his gun hand. He moved to draw the Beretta 93-R.

Rook's left arm snapped out and Bolan felt a cold line drawn across his chest. The cold turned to heat and Bolan could feel blood welling up, his face flushing as his body processed the injury it had received. The small, bloody, leaf-shaped blade in Rook's hand was attached to a miniature pistol grip—a Ka-Bar TDI knife, popular with law enforcement as a backup tool.

Rook stepped in and kicked; metal scraped across the linoleum floor. Bolan's hand reached for the Beretta in its custom rig and found nothing but torn leather. He realized then that Rook's razor-sharp blade had not been meant to injure him, but to cut free the pistol.

Rook hopped forward and lunged.

Bolan stomped on Rook's good hand with a low side kick. It snapped.

Screaming, Rook folded onto himself, still holding the knife. Bolan dropped forward, driving his knees and all his weight into his opponent's abdomen. The man vomited violently as Bolan rolled off him, yanking the combat knife from his blacksuit's combat harness. He brought it around and down, plunging the knife into Rook's subclavian artery as he knelt over the broken vigilante, ending the fight once and for all as he jerked the blade back and forth.

Rook screamed and clutched at Bolan. He reached for the second Smith & Wesson pistol in his waistband behind his back. He could not quite reach it.

Bolan watched him struggle feebly until he died, his eyes glassy, staring at nothing in dilated horror.

Mack Bolan stood, leaving the knife lodged in Gary Rook's body. He looked down at the fallen vigilante for a long moment. This was, or had been, evil. This was the result when men took vengeance one step too far, when they did not care whom they hurt or killed in the pursuit of their justice. Bolan bent and closed Rook's eyes, leaving the fallen soldier, the broken man, to whatever awaited him on the other side of his revenge.

As the Executioner walked down the paved path from the front doors of Station 8, he signaled the police and blacksuits behind the barricade. "It's clear," he said. "The hostages are still inside." They flowed past him, to attend to Rook's former prisoners and to secure the area. There would be no end to the paperwork some of them would fill out this day, Bolan imagined. He found Jack Grimaldi standing by the rented SUV, grinning and shaking his head, clearly glad to see him.

"I have to hand it to you, Sarge," he said. "I was sitting in the truck at the time and almost dropped my coffee. That was a one-in-one-hundred shot."

Bolan followed Grimaldi's gaze. The bullet from Rook's pistol had punched a hole through the center of the SUV's windshield.

16

Washington, D.C.

Brognola was seated behind his desk, several files open on his computer, when the pair of Secret Service agents let themselves in. They came unannounced and they barely looked at him except to nod, acknowledging his presence. One of them held the door as their charge entered the room.

"Hal," his visitor said, extending a hand.

"Mr. Vice President." Brognola stood, taking the proffered hand in a strong grip.

"I've read your preliminary memo," the vice president said. "The President and I have conferred and I'll be meeting with the secretaries of defense and state later this afternoon."

"It is disturbing," Brognola agreed, "but, if you'll permit me, sir, not terribly surprising."

"I agree," the vice president said.

"I'll have the complete briefing from my team later today, I believe," Brognola promised.

"Will it tell me anything we don't already suspect?"

"Not in the broad details, sir," Brognola admitted.

The vice president circled Brognola's desk and stood at the window, looking out, his hands behind his back as he took in the vista. Washington sprawled before him.

"We have to handle this delicately," he said finally. "The nation cannot afford a war with Communist China at this time."

"Nor they with us," Brognola offered.

"I don't like this, Hal," the vice president admitted. "I don't like covering this up for the greater good."

"Nor do I, sir," Brognola stated. "But we've gained vital intelligence. My people are on it and will stay on it. If they try to hit us, we will know. We will act."

The vice president turned back to Brognola, then nodded to his Secret Service agents. Brognola stood and shook his hand again. He left, one of the agents closing the door quietly as they departed.

Brognola sat and half swiveled in his chair to look at Washington, reaching for a bottle of antacids that he kept in his desk drawer. The city outside was deceptively peaceful.

Stony Man Farm, Virginia

"THANK EVERYONE FOR their help," Bolan told Barbara Price over the scrambled phone. "I'm sending Jack back to you, none the worse for wear. His borrowed Cobra fared better than my rented SUV."

"I'll do that," Price told him. "Stay safe until I see you."

"You, too."

Closing the connection, Price turned to Kurtzman. "It looks like we can transmit the final report to Hal," she said.

"It's not short." Kurtzman shook his head. He looked to Akira Tokaido, who had the data compiled and ready to encrypt and send.

"Roger Kohler, desperate for cash, augmented his income by trafficking in drugs, which he did with the help of local gang muscle," Tokaido summarized. "That gang was the target of Gary Rook, who was murdering members of the gang in revenge for the death of his daughter, a meth addict. Striker arrived on the scene to investigate the collateral damage Rook was causing and was mistaken by the gang members for Rook. The gang proceeded to target Striker for elimination, with disastrous results."

"Sounds right so far," Price commented.

"Kohler brokered a deal with General Cao Chang to sell him a large supply of methamphetamine," Tokaido continued. "He thought Chang was a simple criminal syndicate figure, but Chang was actually working as an agent of his government in a plan to destabilize American society through a terrorist attack or attacks. Chang had a formula to create homegrown nerve gas from crystal meth. He was going to target a political gathering at a local college, assassinating a United States senator in the bargain. He planned to make it look like the work of a domestic terrorist group, based on what we know from the backtracing we've done."

"Kohler was found mysteriously dead in his home, removing him from the picture. Shots were fired through his bedroom door, so we assume he was murdered. By whom remains a mystery. The sleeper agent murdered at least one employee that we know about. He got spooked when a local questioned him about it, fled and was pursued. The local turned out to be an armed citizen who shot the sleeper agent dead when the agent tried to fight his way to freedom."

"Only in America." Kurtzman chuckled.

"Striker and Jack hit Chang's safehouse in Ithaca—" Tokaido wrapped up his summary "—then followed up at Chang's offices. The man himself escaped and is probably on his way back to China by now. The vigilante, meanwhile, resurfaced in Syracuse after breaking police custody and fighting his way out of a coma. He took hostages at a local police station in order to get out his message, for whatever reason, which is when Striker came down on him and ended the affair."

"A fairly neat package," Price commented, "with two loose ends. One, we know the Chinese government is actively working against the United States."

"Not exactly a surprise," Kurtzman commented. "This won't be the last we hear from them."

"Two," Price continued, "Cao Chang is still at large and probably beyond our grasp. Update his files accordingly and flag him as a person of interest. If we have the chance in the future, we *will* take him out. That's all, people. Take a break—you've earned it."

Kurtzman, wheeling himself from the room, stopped to look back at Price.

"Do you really think we'll even get the chance, Barb?" he said.

"Not really," she told him.

Kurtzman nodded. He wheeled off, leaving Price alone with her thoughts.

JAMES AXLER

DEATH LANDS®

Sunspot

The land around the Rio Grande reaches the breaking point in a bitter war with an old enemy whose secret stockpile of twenty-first-century nerve gas is poised to unleash infinite madness once more upon a ravaged earth. Can Ryan save the ville from the potential destruction?

Available in December wherever books are sold.

ROOM 59

CRISIS: A massive armed insurgency—
ninety miles off America's coast.

MISSION: CUBA

A Cuban revolution threatens to force the U.S.
into a dangerous game of global brinksmanship,
thrusting spymaster Jonas Schrader into an
emotional war zone—exacting the highest price
for a mission completed.

Look for

THE powers THAT be

by cliff RYDER

GOLD EAGLE®

GRM591